# Who's Afraid of
## Sixth Grade?

# Who's Afraid of Sixth Grade?

by Janet Adele Bloss

Cover illustration by Bill Robison

Published by Willowisp Press, Inc.
401 E. Wilson Bridge Road, Worthington, Ohio 43085

Printed in the United States of America
10 9 8 7 6 5 4 3

ISBN 0-87406-029-X

*To Aunt Gerry,*
*Aunt Helen,*
*Aunt Mary Evelyn,*
*and*
*Uncle Leslie*

# ONE

IT was a sunny day in Duncan, Missouri. Duncan Elementary School had closed just one week earlier, and now the summer months stretched ahead. Eleven-year-old Skye Johnson sat in the green grass of her front yard, waiting for her friends to come over. Skye was having a slumber party to celebrate the end of fifth grade and the beginning of summer. Her best friend, Lizzie Stutz, was the first to arrive.

"Hi, Skye," Lizzie called as she bicycled up into the driveway. "Who else is coming?" She parked her bike and removed her backpack.

Skye jumped up and brushed the grass from her knees. "Amy and Nel are coming," she said. "Nel's bringing her new albums. I can't wait to hear them."

"How's the tennis coming?" asked Lizzie.

"Okay. I played Mom this morning and we

7

almost tied. She was pretty worried there for a while," Skye laughed. "I slammed a few serves right by her."

Skye loved to play tennis. Her mother had played in college and had taught Skye to play as soon as Skye was old enough to hold a racket. Skye's seventeen-year-old brother, Bill, played tennis, too. Skye thought Bill wasn't as much fun to play with as her mom. When Skye played tennis with Bill, he laughed and hooted every time she missed the ball. He yelled things like, "Hey, Skye! Is there a hole in your racket?" It made her mad when he laughed.

When he said things like that, Skye got so flustered that she started missing even the easy balls.

A brown station wagon pulled up in front of the house. Amy and Nel climbed out of the backseat with their sleeping bags and overnight cases. "Bye, Mom," called Amy as her mother drove off.

"Hi, Skye. Hi, Lizzie. Who else is coming?" asked Nel.

"This is it," said Skye. "Billy Count couldn't make it. He has a cold." She grinned at her friends.

"Yeah, right," said Lizzie. "I'm sure. You and Billy are real good friends, huh?"

"That's right," giggled Skye. "You know

how I get along with all the rock stars."

"You wish," said Nel. "I have his album right here if you want to listen to it." She patted her overnight case. "It's even better than his last one. Wait until you see his picture on the cover. Wow! What a hunk!"

"He's so cute," sighed Amy.

"Dream on, girls," said Lizzie. "I don't think Billy Count would look twice at sixth-grade girls."

"That's right. We're in the sixth grade, now," said Skye. "That seems so old, doesn't it? What do you think it's going to be like next year at the middle school?"

"I don't even want to think about it," admitted Nel with a frown. "We'll be *the* youngest kids in the middle school. Yuk. I wonder what the seventh and eighth graders will be like."

"I bet they hate sixth graders," moaned Skye. "Probably they think we're still wearing diapers." She shook her head sadly.

"Oh, come on, Skye," exclaimed Lizzie. "It can't be *that* bad in the middle school."

"I don't know," said Nel. "I've heard that the eighth graders make the new sixth graders carry their books to class for them."

"And sometimes they make the sixth graders eat worms from science class," said

Skye, making a horrible face.

"Oh, Skye. Give me a break," laughed Lizzie. "Who told you that?"

"Bill," said Skye. "He said that back when he was in middle school they treated the sixth graders like garbage. I'm not kidding. That's what he said."

"If you believe everything your older brother says, you're in BIG trouble," said Lizzie. She nodded her head wisely. "Brothers are like cats," she said. "You have to know when to ignore them."

The four girls sat in the grass. It tickled the backs of their legs. Nel and Amy leaned against their sleeping bags.

"How old is your brother?" Nel asked, turning to Skye.

"He's seventeen. He'll be a high school senior next year. You'd think he was going to be President of the United States from the way he acts," Skye said, crossing her eyes. "He keeps asking me if I have a bra yet. How gross can you get?"

"Marty Carroll doesn't have one yet," said Lizzie. "Neither does Edith Schwarzman."

"Oh, great," said Skye. "That makes me feel a lot better. Me and two nerds are the only girls in sixth grade who don't have bras."

"Well, you don't know about the girls from

the other elementary school," said Nel. "Some of them might not wear bras."

"Union Elementary?" asked Skye. "That's a private school. All those girls will wear bras for sure. I'll put money on it."

"Even if they do wear bras, those girls are probably just as scared as we are," said Lizzie. "After all, they'll be in the same class with us. They'll be new at the middle school, too."

"Yeah, but they're all rich," said Nel. "They wear really neat clothes."

"Some of them hang out at the pool," said Amy. "You should see the bathing suits they wear. My mom would kill me if I wore something like that. Some of them look like they're made out of handkerchiefs. They're beautiful," she sighed.

The four girls peered down the road when they heard the sound of clanking and rattling. Clankety-clankety-clankety came the sound of metal and gears. A puff of smoke came into view.

"Bill's home," said Skye, rolling her eyes.

"What's he driving?" asked Lizzie. "A steamroller?"

"That's his new car," Skye said with a laugh. "He just got it. He bought it with two hundred dollars he saved from working at the Pizza House. He's crazy about it. He calls the car

'Emmie'. Is that weird, or what?"

A blue car with a yellow top crested the hill and pulled jerkily into the Johnsons' driveway. The car coughed and shook as a teenaged boy opened the driver's door and climbed out.

"Hi, Bill," Nel called as she stood up.

"Bill, you forgot to turn your car off," said Skye.

"It *is* off," said Bill. "Emmie here just likes to dance a little bit. That's all. She dances for a second, then she stops."

"That's weird," said Skye. "I thought cars were supposed to stop moving when you turned them off."

"Emmie looks more like she's dying than dancing," giggled Lizzie.

Bill patted the car's hood. "Good ol' girl," he said. "Don't listen to them. They're just babies. They don't know what they're talking about."

"Oh, be quiet," said Skye. "Give us a break."

Bill stuck his hands in his pockets and strolled over. "Hey, Skye," he said. "You wearing a bra yet?"

Skye felt her face flush pink as she glared at her brother. This was the thousandth time that he'd asked the same question, and it always embarrassed her.

"What's the matter, Skye?" asked Bill. "Don't you want to be the only girl next year who isn't wearing a bra?"

Skye sat up straight in the grass, determined that Bill wasn't going to get the best of her this time. "What's this thing you have about underwear?" she asked. "You seem to talk about girls' underwear a lot. Do you have some kind of problem I don't know about?"

Bill started to laugh. He turned to the other three girls and said, "Skye is scared to death about going into sixth grade in a new school next year. I'll bet you girls aren't afraid though, are you? You probably won't mind eating worms and wearing your pajamas to class, will you? Did you know that that's what they make the sixth graders do?"

"Get lost," said Skye. "You bore me."

Bill jumped back in mock surprise. "I'm getting some hostile vibes here," he said. "I think I'd better leave before you girls get violent." With a laugh, he turned and walked into the house.

"See what I mean?" asked Skye.

"I think he's neat," said Nel dreamily as she sat down in the grass again.

"Well, he's not. He's awful. Next he'll be asking me if I've started my period."

"You haven't, have you?" asked Nel.

"No," admitted Skye. "You guys haven't started yet either, have you?" she asked with a note of worry in her voice.

"Nope," said Nel.

"Not yet," said Amy.

"Judy has," said Lizzie. "I don't care if I never do. I think it sounds like a pain."

"Judy says it's neat," said Nel.

"People with periods are weird," said Skye. "It's like they're members of the Period Club or something. Let's all make a pact that we won't get weird when start our periods. Okay?"

"That's okay with me," said Lizzie. "I won't get weird. I promise." She held out her hand. The other girls put their hands on top of hers and said, "We promise we won't get weird when we start our periods." Then they all looked at each other and fell back into the grass, giggling.

"Oh, no! It's too late. We're *already* weird," choked Skye through her laughter. "I hope we're not too weird for the boys at the middle school. The seventh and eighth graders probably won't even talk to us." She paused. "I wonder what the sixth-grade guys from Union are like. Do you know any of the boys from the middle school?" asked Skye.

"One lives on my street," said Lizzie. "His name's Kurt Freeman. He's in seventh grade and he's really cute. But I don't think he knows who I am. I think he's going steady with some girl in his own grade. We won't stand a chance with all those older girls."

"The boys in our class are already acting weird around the girls from Union Elementary," added Nel. "They keep showing off for the girls at the pool. They're real hot dogs on the diving board. It's embarrassing. The girls from Union probably think that we're all duds, since our own guys ignore us and show off for them all the time."

"Maybe the guys from Union will show off for *us* if *we* go to the pool. Maybe next year won't be as gross as we think it's going to be," said Skye hopefully.

"Yeah, and maybe we'll all change into movie stars over the summer," snorted Lizzie.

"I'm going to work on my tan," said Skye. "I'm going to start going to the pool after tennis lessons. Who knows? Maybe I'll meet a guy."

"Maybe we'll all be going steady by the time school starts," suggested Nel. "You know, the pool is a pretty good place to meet guys. We should start going there more often."

"You guys sound like you'll die if you don't

have a boyfriend," teased Lizzie. "What happened to the good old days when we used to yell and throw mudballs at them?"

"I never did that," said Skye.

"Me either," said Nel.

"Oh," said Lizzie. "Well anyway, there's got to be something more important than boys."

"I'll let you know if I think of anything," said Skye with a grin. Her brown eyes flashed as they caught the bright June sun. She ran her fingers through her short, black hair and stared up at the white clouds passing overhead.

"Wow!" Nel said. "In just three months, we'll all be at a new school."

"Yeah," moaned Lizzie. "And we'll be the youngest kids in the whole school, too."

"I just hope they don't make sixth graders eat worms," said Skye.

# TWO

"SKYE, where are you going?" Barbara Johnson asked. "Did you clean your room like I asked you to?"

"Yeah, Mom," said Skye. "I'm meeting Lizzie at the pool. I'll ride my bike there."

Skye's mother looked worried. "Maybe you could get Bill to drive you. Isn't that too far for you to ride your bike?"

"No, Mom," Skye said with a sigh. "I'll be okay. It's not that far."

"I don't know, dear. The traffic gets pretty heavy near the pool, doesn't it?" Mrs. Johnson sounded concerned.

"Don't worry, Mom. I've ridden my bike there before. It's not bad."

"Okay, honey. Just be sure and get home in time for dinner." She gave her daughter a hug and added, "By the way, the petunia garden needs to be weeded sometime today."

"Okay," groaned Skye. "I'll do it when I get back." Skye stuffed a beach towel and swimsuit into her backpack and slid the straps onto her shoulders. She walked out of the house, hopped onto her bike, and began pedaling. As she rode down the street, she thought to herself, Sheesh! What am I, a baby or something? I'm eleven years old! Why does Mom treat me like I'm three? When is she going to figure out that I'm old enough to take care of myself?

Skye turned onto Duncan's main road. Cars passed her. Store fronts lined the street. She pedaled by the bank, then by the park. Skye was always proud when she passed the park because she knew that her father had been the one to put the park together. Skye's father, Ed Johnson, was a town planner. He worked with a group of other men and women to decide what was best for the town of Duncan. They decided which parts of the town should have businesses in them, and which parts should be just for homes and families.

The park had been Mr. Johnson's own idea. He'd said, "I think Duncan needs a park where the children can play, and where the older folks can take walks and feel safe." The other town planners agreed with him. So, they raised the money and built the park. The park was made up of several acres of green lawn with clusters of trees here and there. A small playground was at one end of the park, while picnic tables and benches were at the other end.

Skye rode by. As she drew closer to the pool, she began to worry about whether or not Lizzie was already there. Hopefully, she was. Skye dreaded the thought of being alone. This was a pool where a lot of the Union Elementary kids hung out. Also, some of the older kids from the middle school came here to swim, lie in the sun, and flirt with each other.

Skye stood up on the pedals and pumped her legs harder as she began climbing the hill to the pool. She heard splashing and laughter in the distance. She parked her bike and walked through the gate. Looking around, she saw groups of kids, but not Lizzie.

Skye went to the girls' dressing room where she changed into her swimsuit. She was glad that no one else was in there to see that she wasn't wearing a bra under her T-shirt. At least, the top of her two-piece was like a bra. Skye tied it in the back and stepped in front of a big mirror. Her suit was purple and looked nice against her golden-tanned skin. She turned to the side and gazed at her body in the mirror. It was slender, muscular, and straight. "Oh, pooh!" she muttered to herself. "When am I going to grow? I look like a boy."

"No, you don't. You look like a girl to me," came a voice from around the corner.

Skye jumped back with surprise. Then she laughed. "Darn it, Lizzie!" she said. "Don't sneak up on me like that."

"Sorry," said Lizzie with a smile. "I saw you over here talking to yourself in the mirror, and I couldn't resist. Are you still worried about your breasts? You know, you shouldn't be. My mom says that different girls start to grow at different times."

"I know," said Skye. "That's what our health teacher said at school. But, everyone's breasts are growing except for mine. I feel like a freak."

"What's wrong with being a freak?" laughed Lizzie. "Some of my best friends are freaks." She winked at Skye.

Skye stared at herself again in the mirror. "Maybe I could wear my swimsuit top under my clothes all the time, and everyone would think it was a bra," she said.

"Yeah, a bright purple bra," laughed Lizzie. "Come on. Let's get out into the sun. It's dark in here."

Skye and Lizzie left the dressing room and

walked out onto the cement by the pool. Skye looked around for someone she knew, but there were just a few boys from Duncan Elementary. All of the other kids were strangers. Skye thought that the other kids were probably from Union Elementary.

"How about right here?" asked Lizzie, spreading her towel on some grass next to the cement. Skye lay her towel on the ground, then sat on it. The June sun beat down and Skye began to feel her skin tingle in the heat.

"Hey! There's Kurt Freeman," whispered Lizzie, pointing to a blond boy in red trunks. "He's the guy that I was telling you about who lives on my street. He's in seventh grade."

"Don't point!" whispered Skye. "He'll think we're talking about him."

"We are," chuckled Lizzie. "Ready for a swim? It's too hot out here. I'm going in the water."

"I think I'll wait," said Skye. "I have to get some sun on my back. My front is tanned, but my back is white. It's gross." She flipped over onto her stomach and faced the pool with her chin on her hands. Lizzie stood up and walked to the diving board. She dived into the pool. She swam its length underwater emerging in the shallow end, and then began swimming laps.

Skye reached for her sunglasses. She thought summertime was great. She could stare at people from behind sunglasses and they never knew it. There's only one problem, Skye thought with a smile. If you wear sunglasses too long, the tan on your face gets messed up. Little white lines leading from your eyes to your ears run across your face. But sunglasses sure do come in handy when you secretly want to watch people.

Skye turned her head to one side. She noticed a red-haired girl in a yellow bikini. Wow! thought Skye. She's cute, and she has a tennis racket lying on her towel beside her. Skye wondered who she was. She looked like the sort of girl who had a million boyfriends and made straight A's. Skye wondered if she could beat this red-haired girl in tennis.

Kurt Freeman walked over to the red-haired girl. He squeezed a bottle of suntan oil over her back and the cold lotion fell in drops. "Eeee-eeee! Kurt, you jerk!" she laughed. She picked up a magazine and threw it at him, just missing his shoulder.

"Calm down, Marcia," said Kurt. He pretended to be afraid by putting his hands up in front of his face.

Skye watched from behind her sunglasses.

"Skye!" Lizzie called from the pool. "Come

on in. I'll race you the length of the pool!"

Skye sat up and took off her glasses. "Why not?" she called back. Skye was getting bored just sitting by the pool. She wondered if more boys would talk to her if she had red hair and wore a yellow bikini. She stood up and walked toward the diving board. Skye saw Kurt Freeman look up as she walked by. A group of the Union boys were treading water in the pool. They watched her as she climbed the steps to the diving board.

Skye glanced down at her tan body and purple two-piece. She poised near the edge of the board. She took one step and bounced upward. She dived gracefully into the water. As soon as her shoulders hit the water, Skye felt it happen. The straps of her purple top pulled loose and floated away on a rush of water. Skye felt the cold water on her bare chest as she swam underwater. She wondered what to do.

Skye thought that this had to be the most embarrassing moment of her life! Here she was, surrounded by cute boys from Union Elementary, and she was swimming in only *one-half* of a *two*-piece suit. Skye continued to swim underwater, afraid that if she came up for air, she'd hear everyone laughing at her. Her cheeks and eyes bulged as she struggled to hold her breath for just a little longer.

At last Skye came to the surface. She saw Lizzie standing in the shallow end, her mouth round with surprise. She was pointing back at Skye's top floating under the diving board. Skye took a deep breath and dived underwater, keeping her eyes open. When she spotted the purple top above her, she came to the surface and grabbed it.

"Hey, Skye! Did you lose something?" called Todd Kennedy from the side of the pool. Skye quickly slid her arms into the suit top and tied the strings behind her back. She glared at Todd who smiled back at her.

"Hey, Skye! I like your swimsuit," called Todd again. "Is that a new style?" Skye could hear Todd laughing.

Skye ignored Todd and swam to the shallow end. She joined Lizzie who stood with a shocked look on her face. "Boy!" said Lizzie. "That was some dive!"

"I think I'm going to die," whispered Skye. "I'm so-o-o embarrassed."

"Don't worry about it," said Lizzie. "I don't see what the big deal is about seeing someone's chest. Everybody has one."

"That's easy for you to say," moaned Skye. "You didn't just leave your bikini floating in the deep end while *you* were swimming in the shallow end. It wasn't *your* chest that everyone was staring at."

"Don't worry. *Everyone* wasn't staring at you," said Lizzie.

"They weren't?" asked Skye hopefully.

"Nah." Lizzie shook her head. "The girls didn't notice a thing. It was just the boys who watched you." Lizzie smiled. "Sorry, Skye. I'm just kidding. Really. Hardly anyone saw."

"Todd Kennedy saw," said Skye with a frown.

"He doesn't count," Lizzie said reassuringly. "He's such a nerd. Come on. Let's get out of the pool and get some sun."

"No way!" whispered Skye emphatically. "I'm not getting out of this pool for anything! Then I'd have to walk by everyone and they'd stare at me."

"Well, we just can't stand here whispering forever," insisted Lizzie. "I'm getting cold. I have to move or I'll freeze. I have an idea. Let's race!"

"I don't know," said Skye doubtfully. "What if everyone stares at me and laughs?"

"They'll laugh even more if you stand down here forever and wrinkle up like a raisin," said Lizzie.

"I guess you're right," admitted Skye. She tugged the back of her swimsuit top to make sure it was securely tied. "I could just die!" she mumbled to herself. "I'll never live this down. I'll be known forever as 'the topless swimmer'."

"Quit feeling sorry for yourself," chided Lizzie. "Come on. Let's race!" Lizzie dived into the water and Skye followed a split second later.

The two girls swam furiously toward the other end of the pool. Lizzie beat Skye by a frog's hair as her fingers touched the edge.

"Let's do it again," said Skye. The two girls turned and raced toward the other end. "Ouch!" yelled Skye. She banged into a body in the middle of the pool. She swallowed some water and stood up sputtering.

"Oh, excu-u-u-use me," said Todd Kennedy sarcastically. "I didn't mean to get in your way. I didn't know this was *your* pool."

"What are you talking about?" asked Skye, wiping the water from her face.

"I'm talking about that great dive you made a minute ago," said Todd.

"You're weird," said Skye, frowning. She dived into the water beside Todd and swam away, kicking the water as hard as she could. She could hear Todd coughing behind her.

She swam up to Lizzie. "Was Todd bugging you?" asked Lizzie.

"Yeah," said Skye, shaking with anger.

"He's such a jerk," said Lizzie. "Just ignore him. Are you ready to get out of the pool now?"

"Yeah, I guess so," said Skye. "I think I can handle it. But I swear, if anyone laughs at me, I'm moving to Alaska and never coming back."

"I'll miss you," said Lizzie with a grin. "Come on. Let's get out of here." She swam to the pool ladder and climbed out with Skye right behind her.

Returning to their towels, Lizzie said, "See? No one laughed."

"What a relief!" exclaimed Skye. "Say, do you know that girl over there in the yellow suit?"

Lizzie looked. "No, I don't think so," she said. "Why?"

"Well, I think she's from Union Elementary," said Skye. "All I know about her is that her name's Marcia."

"Oh!" exclaimed Lizzie. "That must be Marcia Glanders. I've heard of her. She's our age and she's real popular. We'll be in the same class next year."

"There's her racket," said Skye. "She must play tennis. I wonder if she's any good."

"She looks pretty athletic," said Lizzie. "But why do you care?"

"I don't know," said Skye. "I was just wondering about her, that's all."

"You can get to know her better next year if you want to," suggested Lizzie. "Or you could go over right now and introduce yourself."

"Yeah. Good idea," said Skye. She looked at the clock over the concession stand. "Uh oh," she exclaimed. "It's 4:30. I have to get home. Don't forget, I'm playing tennis with Bill tomorrow. So I'll be here later in the afternoon. Are you coming to the pool?"

"Probably," said Lizzie.

"Okay. I'll see you tomorrow. Bye." Skye rolled up her towel and walked toward the girls' dressing room. Was it her imagination or was Kurt Freeman staring at her from across the pool? She wondered.

On her way home, Skye pedaled as fast as she could. She had to get home in time to pull the weeds out of the petunia garden before dinner. She glanced down at her feet going around and around on the pedals. That's funny, she thought. I've never really noticed my feet before. But now that she looked at them, they seemed bigger than usual. In fact, they seemed larger than the feet of a normal eleven-year-old girl. "Oh, that's just great," Skye muttered to herself. "All of my growing juices are going to my feet. The rest of my body is flat as a board, but my feet are growing like balloons. I'll be real popular next year at the middle school. People will say, 'Hey! There goes Skye Johnson. Wow! Have you seen her feet? She sure has some big ones!'"

Bl-a-a-ahhh! The sound of a car horn almost made Skye lose her balance. A puff of black smoke reached her nose. She looked over her shoulder to see a blue and yellow car behind her. Bill sat smiling behind the wheel. He leaned toward the passenger-side window as he passed her. "Hey, squirt!" he called. "Sixth graders aren't allowed to ride bikes on this road. Didn't you know that?" Bill laughed out loud. He and Emmie noisily pulled ahead of Skye and disappeared over the next hill in the road.

"Oh, wow!" Skye muttered to herself again. "Not only do I have elephant feet, but I also have a brother who belongs in a zoo." She glanced down at her feet. Then she looked ahead at the gray cloud of smoke that Bill had left in the road. Skye sighed and shook her head. "Big feet and a bozo brother. Unfortunately, I think I'm stuck with both of them," she said to herself. Skye stood on the pedals and pumped as hard as she could, heading for home and a weedy petunia garden.

# THREE

BILL smiled happily as he served the ball. "30-Love," he said. He smashed his racket down onto the ball, causing it to fly over the net onto Skye's court. She hit the ball with her racket and sent it spinning back to Bill's side. It whizzed past him as he reached for it. "Darn!" he said. "You have a point. Good one, Skye. Now the score's 30-15."

"Bill, do you know why they call zero 'love' in tennis? It seems weird. Since it's zero, why isn't it called zero?" asked Skye.

"Yeah, it is kind of weird," said Bill. "They call it 'love' because tennis is a French game. *L'oeuf* means 'the egg' in French, and an egg is round like a zero. *L'oeuf* sounds like 'love' and that's what everyone started calling it." He leaned over and picked up two balls. "Come on, sis. Let's play."

Bill served the ball and Skye hit it back to

him. Then he yelled, "Look behind you! The Martians are coming!"

Skye jumped at the sound of his voice, and the ball flew past her.

"My point," said Bill. "It's 40-15, ad in."

"That's not fair," said Skye hotly. "If we were in a tournament, they'd throw you out for cheating. It's not fair to yell at the other player."

"Sure, it's fair," said Bill. "That's your problem if you believe in Martians."

"I don't believe in Martians," insisted Skye. "But I do believe in jerky brothers. Why can't you ever play a game of tennis like a normal person?"

"Because I'm not a normal person," said Bill, screwing up his mouth and crossing his eyes. Then his face relaxed into a smile. "Come on, Skye," he said. "Don't take everything so seriously. Can't you take a joke?"

"Sure. When it's funny," said Skye. She wondered to herself, Why does Bill always have to give me a hard time? Are all big brothers like this or do I have an unusually bad one?

"Come on, Squirt," said Bill. "Let's play. I have to hurry and beat you so that I can go meet Alex and some of the gang. We're renting motorcycles and riding out into the country this evening."

Skye held her racket tightly in her hand. She was determined to play her best. She'd never beaten Bill before, except for once when he played hopping on one foot. Skye had beaten him then, but it didn't make her feel that good to know that she had to load Bill down with handicaps in order to do it. But maybe today would be different. Maybe she could beat him fair and square.

Bill aimed the ball into the far corner of the court. Skye lunged for it, but fell, scraping her knee on the asphalt surface. "Sorry, Squirt. Just keep working out," said Bill. "Girls don't have the upper body strength that guys have. You need to strengthen your arms."

"What should I do? Lift weights?" asked Skye.

"Sure. You could do that," advised Bill. "Or you can keep up with your swimming," said Bill. "That gives you strong shoulders and should improve your tennis. Swimming is about the best exercise you can get."

Bill collected the tennis balls and put them in their metal container. "Well, I'd better get going. Do you want a ride home?"

"Sure," said Skye. She gathered her tennis gear. They walked over to Emmie in the parking lot. Skye opened the door and slid into the front seat. Bill put his key in the ignition and listened to Emmie's engine cough and splutter. "Good ol' gal," he said. "Come on, Emmie. You can do it, baby. Yeah!" The engine roared, and Emmie jerked into motion. Bill pulled the car out onto the road.

Skye looked at her brother. He seemed so big and strong sitting behind the wheel of the car. "Bill," she said. "Can I ask you a question?"

"Sure," said Bill. "Shoot."

"What's sixth grade like? I mean, when you started going to the middle school, were you afraid?"

"Me? Afraid? You have to be kidding!" joked Bill. "I've never been afraid of anything in my whole life." Suddenly, his face looked serious. "I probably should have been afraid, though, now that I think about it," he said. "Sixth grade was a lot like going to prison. All the seventh and eighth graders in the middle school are mean and nasty. All they think about is picking on the sixth graders. If you don't watch out, they'll make you walk backward to class. I remember one sixth grader in my class named Tammy Winkle. One of the eighth graders made her climb the flag pole. Poor Tammy sat up there for three weeks.

"Oh, give me a break," said Skye.

"It's true," said Bill. "Cross my heart."

"You're such a liar," said Skye.

"Why, thank you," said Bill, tipping an imaginary hat. "Here we are." He pulled the complaining Emmie into the driveway. "Tell Mom I'll be home after dinner," Bill called to Skye as she climbed out of the car. "Bye!" He backed out and drove away.

Skye thought, It must be nice to come and go whenever you want. I can't wait until I'm seventeen years old. Bill has a lot more freedom than I do. That's not fair.

Skye walked into the house and found her mother cutting up tomatoes for a salad. "Hi, honey," said Barbara Johnson. "It's almost time for dinner. Would you please set the table?"

"Bill won't be here for dinner," said Skye. "You know, Mom. It seems like I'm kind of a slave around here. How come I have to set the table, and Bill's off with his friends?"

Mrs. Johnson wiped her hands on her apron and looked at Skye. "I'm sorry you feel like a slave," she said. "Bill used to set the table every night when you were too young to help. He used to complain about it all the time, too," she said with a sigh. "How about if you two work out a table-setting schedule where you take turns?" she suggested.

"That sounds okay," said Skye agreeably. "Would you talk to Bill? He never listens to me."

"I'll talk to him," agreed Mrs. Johnson. "By the way, how did your tennis game go? Have you skunked Bill yet?"

"Not yet. But I plan to before this summer is over," said Skye with determination.

Skye heard the phone ring and ran to answer it. "Hello?" she said. Then she held the receiver against her chest saying, "Mom, it's Lizzie. I'll talk to her upstairs. Hang up when I get on, okay?"

Mrs. Johnson nodded. Skye ran out of the kitchen and upstairs to the private phone in her bedroom. It was a present for her eleventh birthday. The pink phone matched the pink-flowered wallpaper in her room. She picked up the receiver. "Okay, Mom. You can hang up," she said. There was a clicking noise and Lizzie said, "Hi, Skye. What's happening?"

"Not much," said Skye. "What's happening with you?"

"Not much." There were a few moments of silence and then Lizzie said, "I don't know about you, but I'm bored. Summers are great when they first start. But, once you get into them, they seem to last forever." She sighed and then continued, "I didn't see you at the pool today. Where were you?"

"I ended up playing tennis with Bill for most of the afternoon," said Skye.

"Did you . . . ?" asked Lizzie.

"No," interrupted Skye. "He beat me every time. What a drag! If I keep this up, maybe I can get into the *Guinness Book of World Records* for the person who's lost the most games of tennis to her brother."

"Well, what do you expect?" asked Lizzie. "He's bigger and older than you. Whenever you play anyone your own age, you usually smear them all over the court." She laughed. "I ought to know. You've smeared me before."

"I know," said Skye. "But I wish I was better. Was anyone interesting at the pool today?" she asked. She stretched back onto her pink ruffled bed, holding the receiver to her ear.

"The usual people," said Lizzie. "Marcia Glanders was there in a really cute pink bikini. All the guys were flirting with her and acting like real jerks."

"Was Kurt Freeman there?" asked Skye.

"Yeah. He was there with some of the other seventh-grade guys. They kept throwing girls into the pool."

"Did they throw you in?" asked Skye.

"Are you kidding?" exclaimed Lizzie. "They tried. But I wrapped my legs around one of them and my arms around another. They couldn't pry me loose. Finally they gave up."

Skye started to giggle uncontrollably.

"What's so funny?" asked Lizzie.

"Oh, I can just picture you," said Skye. "I'll bet you looked like a big pretzel made out of arms and legs. Most girls would just go along with it and let the guys throw them in. They'd think it was fun. But not *you*. *You* have to put up a fight."

"Darn right!" said Lizzie, laughing. "I figure I'll go into the pool when I'm good and ready. I don't need a bunch of bozos throwing me in."

"Were there any new guys?" asked Skye.

"I didn't see any," said Lizzie. "Nel and Amy came by for a little while. Amy kept talking about some Union guy with brown hair almost down to his shoulders. She thought he was real cute. But he didn't look so special to me. He wasn't any big deal. Are you coming to the pool tomorrow? It's real boring without you there."

"I'm going to try to make it," said Skye. "But first, Mom and I are going shopping. Bevie's is having a sale on back-to-school clothes."

"Good grief! Summer just started. It's kind

of early for that, isn't it?" asked Lizzie.

"Nah. If I'm going to compete with those Union girls next year, I'd better start shopping now."

"I wonder what it'll be like next year?" mused Lizzie.

"I don't know," said Skye. "But one thing's for sure."

"What's that?" asked Lizzie.

Skye breathed deeply into the phone. "If I don't have a bra by the time school starts, I might as well move to another state. I don't think I could handle it. Also, there's something else on my mind."

"What's that?"

"Promise you won't laugh?" asked Skye.

"I promise," said Lizzie.

"I haven't talked about this with anyone else," said Skye. "Don't tell anyone, not even Amy or Nel." She paused and took a deep breath. "I'm worried about my feet," she said. "I think they're growing faster than the rest of me. In fact, I've been kind of worried that playing tennis is making them bigger." She paused and took a deep breath. "Tell me the truth. Have you noticed anything weird about my feet lately?" Skye frowned and pressed the phone to her ear, waiting for Lizzie's answer.

"Come on, Lizzie," Skye said. "You

promised not to laugh. I'm serious. How would you like it if your feet were beginning to look like big duck feet?"

# FOUR

SKYE'S father folded his newspaper as Skye walked into the room. "I think that dress is my favorite one, so far," he said with a nod. "I think you'll be a smashing success at school tomorrow, Skye. You'll probably have all the boys chasing you home every day."

"Oh, Dad. Give me a break," moaned Skye as she modeled her new back-to-school outfit. "I can't believe the summer is over already!"

"This new school should be quite an adventure for you, eh?" Mr. Johnson reached out and patted Skye's arm. She squirmed away. She knew that her father was just trying to be friendly and nice. But Skye didn't like to be patted. It made her feel like a house pet.

"Yeah, Dad," said Skye. "I guess it'll be an adventure all right. But, what I'm worried about is that it might be a terrible adventure."

"I'm sure you'll do just fine," said Mr.

Johnson. "You'll be riding the bus for the first time, won't you?"

"Yeah," said Skye. "Bill says that the bus driver kicks you off the bus if you don't wear a hat."

"Bill, are you telling stories to your sister?" asked Mr. Johnson, looking sternly at Bill.

Bill was sprawled across the couch in front of the television. "I've been preparing Skye for the real world," said Bill. "I'm just trying to help out, Dad."

"Well, listen here, young man," said Mr. Johnson. "I don't want you 'helping out' by scaring your sister half to death. Understand?"

"Okay," said Bill, grinning. "I won't tell her about what they do to the sixth-grade girls in gym class."

"Bill! Now, I mean it! Quit trying to scare your sister," said Mr. Johnson sternly.

"Okay," said Bill, turning back to the TV.

"Do they really do something to the girls in gym class?" asked Skye.

Her father smiled. "Of course not, honey," he said. "Duncan Middle School is a wonderful facility. I'm sure you'll make lots of new friends there."

"I hope so," said Skye.

Her mother walked into the room holding a red woolen skirt. "I've hemmed this," she said.

"You'd better try it on. If I'd worn skirts this short, my mother would have locked me in the house." She smiled. "Come on, Skye. Don't look so worried. You'll have a lot of your friends from Duncan Elementary with you. It's not as if you'll be completely alone."

The phone rang and it was for Skye. She climbed the stairs two at a time to reach her room. Then she closed the door and lay down on her bed with the phone on her stomach. "Hi, Lizzie," she said. "Are you scared about tomorrow?"

"Yeah," said Lizzie. "I tried not to think about it too much this summer, but now that it's really happening, I have to admit it. I'm scared. At least we get to ride the bus together. You'll get on it before I do, so save me a seat, okay?"

"Okay," said Skye.

"What are you wearing tomorrow?" asked Lizzie.

"It's one of my new outfits. I'll be wearing a red miniskirt and a gray sweater."

"Did your mom get you a you-know-what yet?" asked Lizzie.

"Are you kidding?" sighed Skye. I just *know* I'm going to be the only girl in the whole school still wearing an undershirt, thought Skye. I could just die. "I thought about asking my mom tonight if I could have a bra. But I just couldn't. It's so-o-o embarrassing."

"I know what you mean," said Lizzie. "I'd give you one of mine, but I only have two. That doesn't really leave me with enough to hand out to my friends."

"Oh, well. My sweater's real thick and you can't see through it. Maybe nobody will notice," said Skye hopefully. "Did you know that we're going to have lockers? My number's 124. What's yours?"

"Mine's 186," said Lizzie. "It's going to be weird to have lockers."

"It's going to be even more weird to have classes in different rooms," said Skye. "I wonder what it will be like to change classes. I'm so used to sitting in one room for the whole day."

"This will be more like high school," said Lizzie. "I think it sounds kind of exciting."

"Yeah. It's exciting if you know where you're going," said Skye. "I'll probably get lost in the hall and end up in the wrong classrooms. Probably the teachers will think I look like I'm in second grade and they'll put me on the bus and send me back to Duncan Elementary."

"That's a cheerful thought," said Lizzie.

"I'm sorry," said Skye. "It's just that it's all so new. We're not going to know half of the kids at the middle school. I'm really scared."

"On a scale of one to ten, how scared are you?" asked Lizzie.

"Eleven," said Skye. "The same as my age. I just hope that the seventh and eighth graders aren't as mean as Bill says they are. Yesterday he told me that if you don't eat all of your peas from the school lunch, they make you walk around the halls with a bowl of water on your head. Then if you spill any of the water, the older kids make you lick it off the floor with your tongue."

"You don't believe that, do you?" asked Lizzie.

"Well-l-l, I guess not," said Skye. "But Bill ought to know. He used to go to school there."

"Oh, come on, Skye. Bill's just trying to scare you," Lizzie laughed.

"He's doing a real good job of it," Skye said, trying to laugh.

"Skye!" Mrs. Johnson's voice came from downstairs. "Get off the phone, please. Your father needs to make a call."

"Yeah, Skye," came Bill's voice. "You can talk to Lizzie all night long, but it won't make any difference. You still have to go to a new school tomorrow."

"I have to go," Skye said into the phone.

"Okay. I'll see you on the bus tomorrow.

Don't worry. Everything will be fine. Have some sweet dreams tonight. Try to dream about Kurt Freeman and all of the other cute guys we're going to meet tomorrow. Bye," said Lizzie.

"Bye." Skye hung up the phone and went to the bathroom to brush her teeth. Then she pulled on her pajamas and climbed into bed.

Her mother stuck her head in the door and said, "Goodnight, sweetheart. Don't worry. I know that you'll get along just fine."

"Thanks, Mom," said Skye. "I hope so." Her mother closed the door and Skye was left lying in the dark. She pressed her cheek against her pillow and tried to think about the wonderful things that might happen at the middle school. Maybe I'll meet a cute guy on the very first day, she thought. Maybe I'll make some new girl friends and maybe Lizzie and I will have every single class together. Maybe the teachers will love me and give me easy homework assignments. Or maybe there won't be any homework at all.

Skye smiled as she drifted off into sleep. She dreamed that she was walking down the hall trying to find her locker. There were kids all around her, but the strange thing was that no one was making a sound. All of the kids were watching her as she walked down the hall. With each step she took, her shoes made a loud smacking sound against the floor. Slap-slap-slap! went the soles of her shoes. There were no other sounds. The seventh and eighth graders grinned at her. Then a beautiful red-haired girl in a yellow bikini turned to Kurt Freeman and said, "Look at her feet. Have you ever seen anything so big?"

Skye sat straight up in bed. She looked around herself to make sure that she wasn't still asleep. "It was just a dream," she whispered to herself. "It was just a dream. There's nothing to worry about. Sixth grade is going to be fun." But deep inside, she wasn't so sure.

# FIVE

S KYE sat at the breakfast table with a frown on her face.

"What's the matter, chickadee?" asked her father. "Are you worried about your first day in sixth grade?"

"No," said Skye. She didn't want to admit that she was beyond the worry stage. She was into the scared-to-death stage.

"You look awfully cute this morning," said Mrs. Johnson. She spooned some scrambled eggs onto Skye's plate. "Just relax, honey. The first day is always the worst day. Tomorrow won't be quite so hard."

Skye thought, Why is everyone always giving me advice? I wish everyone would quit acting like they know more than I do. Mom and Dad are too old to remember what it's like to be a kid. They've forgotten how rotten it is to go to a new school for the first time. They wouldn't feel so happy this morning if they were in my shoes. The thought of shoes caused Skye to glance down at her feet. They were under the table in her new shoes, which looked enormous to Skye. She scuffed the side of one shoe against the floor. New shoes are too shiny, she thought. Everyone can spot new shoes a mile away.

"Hey, Squirt!" said Bill, rushing into the kitchen. "So, you're getting thrown to the wolves today, huh?"

Mr. Johnson looked at Bill and raised his eyebrows.

Bill cleared his throat. "Well . . . uh, good morning, Squirt. Good luck at school today."

Mr. Johnson's eyebrows returned to their normal position as he sipped from his coffee cup.

"Hurry, Skye. Your bus will be here any minute," said her mother. "Here's money for lunch. I can start packing a lunch for you if you want me to."

"I want to wait and see what the other kids are doing," said Skye.

"Do you have your new notebooks and your gym bag?" asked Mrs. Johnson.

"Yeah. I have everything," said Skye. She pushed her chair away from the table and pulled a jacket over her sweater. She felt like crying. She wanted to rush back upstairs and hide under her bed. She wanted to lock herself in the bathroom and sit in a tub of nice warm water. She wanted to do *anything* except leave the house and go to a new school. But, she also didn't want her family to know how afraid she was. She wanted them to think that she was old enough to handle going to a new school and riding a bus for the first time. Skye wanted her parents to realize that she was a young lady, not a little girl. Skye also wanted to act brave in front of Bill. Maybe if he thought that she wasn't afraid, then he would quit trying to scare her.

"Bye," called Skye. She opened the kitchen door and stepped out onto the porch. She looked back at her mother, who stood there with worry lines between her eyes.

Skye's father said, "Knock 'em dead, sweetheart!" Bill sat at the table with his hand over his mouth, covering a smile. Skye pulled the door closed behind her and walked down the road to the bus stop.

It was a beautiful September day. A bright blue sky was filled with puffy white clouds. Clear, cold air filled Skye's lungs. Well, there's one good thing that I can count on today, she thought. At least Lizzie will be getting on the bus in just two stops.

Skye heard the sound of a motor and saw a yellow school bus pull into view. Her heart began to beat faster as she noted that the bus carried a group of kids whom she'd never seen before. The bus stopped and Skye climbed the steps to where the bus driver sat. "Hey there, little gal," said the bus driver. "Climb aboard. You don't look like you'll take up much space." He smiled at her.

Skye did not like being called 'little gal'. She wrinkled her nose at the bus driver and walked down the aisle between rows of double seats. Curious eyes stared at her. A rubberband bounced off of her ear and she turned around to see who had shot it. A boy with chubby cheeks grinned up at her. "One point for ears and five points for butts," he said, aiming another rubberband. Skye hurried down the aisle to an empty seat in the back of the bus. She put her notebooks in the empty space next to her in order to save a seat for Lizzie. The bus driver closed the door and drove the bus on down the road.

At the next stop, a group of kids piled onto the bus and began their search for seats. They called to each other.

"Hi, Sarah."

"Hi, Ron. Did you have a good summer?"

"Hey, Paula! What's happening?"

"Smitty! I saved you a seat."

Skye listened to them. It seemed like everyone knew everybody. She was the only person on the bus without a friend.

"Hi, Skye. Mind if I sit here?"

Skye looked up to see Todd Kennedy standing next to her seat. Before she could say a word, he picked her notebooks up and sat down beside her. He was the last person in the world that Skye wanted to see. She hadn't forgotten the time at the pool when the top of her bathing suit fell off, and Todd had embarrassed her.

"I was saving that seat for Lizzie," said Skye.

Todd laughed. "Not anymore you aren't," he said. "Hey! Do you have your class schedule with you? Maybe we have some classes together! Wouldn't that be great?"

"Super," said Skye without enthusiasm. She pressed her forehead against the grimy bus window. The blue autumn sky didn't look so blue through the film of dirt. Skye wondered if they ever washed the buses.

The bus stopped and Skye watched eagerly as more kids climbed on. At last Lizzie walked down the aisle, looking around. "Oh, there you are," said Lizzie, spotting Skye. "I thought you were going to save me a seat. I guess I'll have to sit up here." She walked to the front of the bus.

Skye glared at Todd. "Thanks a lot," she said.

"My pleasure," said Todd, "You know, this is a public bus. You're not allowed to save seats for people." Todd shifted in his seat to look at Skye. "Are you scared about sixth grade?" he asked. "You seem kind of nervous."

"No, I'm not scared," said Skye. "And anyway, it's none of your business." She continued to stare out of the window and ignored Todd for the rest of the ride.

When the bus pulled up beside Duncan Middle School, all of the kids swarmed off the bus. Several students stood around looking a little lost until a teacher came up and said, "All sixth graders should report to the auditorium immediately."

"That would be great if only we knew where the auditorium was," said Lizzie, walking up to Skye. "Hey, how come you didn't save me a seat?"

"I tried," said Skye. "But Todd Kennedy wouldn't leave. He's so obnoxious." She looked around at the other students. "Well, I guess if we just follow the crowd, we'll get to the auditorium."

"Yeah," said Lizzie. "Let's go. Hey! There's Nel!" She waved to Nel, who made her what-are-we-doing-here face.

Skye and Lizzie followed the crowd to the auditorium. They walked into the large room and saw rows and rows of seats. "Can you believe all of the people here?" asked Lizzie.

"Wow!" said Skye. "These are just the sixth graders. I didn't know there would be so many."

"Quiet, please!" shouted a gray-haired woman from the stage in front of the room. "My name is Mrs. Barnhardt and I'm the principal of Duncan Middle School. First of all, I'd like to say welcome to all you sixth graders. I hope you like our school. I encourage you all to learn the rules as soon as possible. I think you'll find that Duncan Middle School is quite a bit different from your elementary school." Mrs. Barnhardt stared at a noisy section of the room until it became completely quiet, then she continued to speak.

"Secondly, I'd like to remind you that we do not allow talking in the halls between classes. We have hall monitors who will watch for talking students. The monitors will give you a pink slip of paper if you are caught talking. They will record your name in a notebook. If anyone gets three pink slips then they will have to come to the main office and talk to me. We will agree upon a suitable punishment at that time. You must also remember to ask your teacher for a blue pass before you leave the classroom for a drink of water or to go to the restroom. If a hall monitor finds you in the hall during class without a pass, your name will be recorded in a notebook and you will have to talk to me after school."

"Is this prison or middle school?" Skye whispered to Lizzie. "They'll probably give you a purple slip if you get caught breathing."

Mrs. Barnhardt continued to talk from the stage. "Please look at your schedules and see where your homeroom is. Then quietly and slowly, please leave the auditorium and go to your lockers. Then go to your homeroom. From now on you will report directly to your homeroom every morning as soon as you enter the school."

Lizzie pulled a piece of paper from her purse. "I'm in 213," she said.

"Oh, pooh!" said Skye. "I'm in 026. That must be the basement." She looked more closely at her schedule. "I can't remember all of these numbers," she whispered. "My locker is 124, and my combination is 37-16-28. My homeroom number is 026. This is confusing.

What time do you have lunch?"

Lizzie looked at her schedule. "Eleven-thirty," she said. "When is yours?"

"Oh, rats! Mine's at twelve-fifteen," moaned Skye. She looked over at Lizzie's schedule, comparing it to her own. "Oh, well. At least we have gym and English together. I guess I'll see you in the gym at one-thirty." Skye stood up and joined the crowd leaving the auditorium. She felt like a cow in a herd of cattle. The kids around her showed eyes wide with worry. They moved slowly, their shoes scraping against the floor. Skye felt like yelling out, "Mooo-o-o!" But she didn't.

It was hard to find her locker with so many kids rushing around the halls. Skye wanted to ask someone for help, but she remembered what Mrs. Barnhardt had said about no talking in the halls. At last, she found her locker. It took five tries at the combination before Skye was able to get the door open. Then she left her books on the shelf, hung her jacket on a hook and began the search for her homeroom. As Skye walked down the hall, she overheard an older boy say to his friend, "Look! The babies are here." Skye felt herself blush.

When she found her homeroom, she walked in and sat down at an empty desk. Looking around, she saw that the other sixth graders in this class were mostly strangers. There were a few people from her old school, but none of them were close friends of hers. As Skye checked out the other students, she realized that one of them looked familiar. Sitting in the first row was the red-haired girl, Marcia Glanders. Marcia was wearing a blue dress and hose and shoes with heels. Skye glanced regretfully down at her own gray knee socks.

"Good morning, class," said a tall man who introduced himself as Mr. Bunn. "I'm your homeroom teacher. Welcome to Duncan Middle School. We don't have much time, so I'll just quickly tell you about some of the rules we have here."

Skye thought, What? More rules? Give me a break. I don't even remember the first set of rules that the principal told us. I'm going to have to get a tape recorder just so I can remember all the different colored slips I'll get if I do something wrong.

"First of all, we don't allow gum chewing in class," said Mr. Bunn. "Anyone who's caught chewing gum will be given a putty knife and a box. They will then go to the auditorium where they will scrape gum off of the chair-bottoms. Also, please remember that you may not leave food in your lockers overnight. It attracts mice."

Just then a wad of paper fell onto Skye's desk. She looked around to see who had thrown it. Gross! she thought. Just two desks behind her sat Todd Kennedy. He smiled at Skye and waved. Skye realized with a frown that he had thrown the note. Skye unfolded the paper and read it. It said, "I know you think I'm a jerk, but I like you anyway. Can I call you tonight?"

Skye stared at the words in disbelief. There is nobody grosser than Todd Kennedy. Of all the people to have a crush on me, Skye thought, why does he have to be the biggest nerd in the history of the world? As Skye stared at the note, she felt her anger rising. Her first day at school was turning into a disaster. First she had to remember eight-million new rules. Then one of the older kids called the sixth graders "babies." And now she had a love note from a boy who always had a dirty handkerchief hanging out of his shirt pocket. It was just too much! Skye crumpled the note up in her hand. She turned around with a terrible frown on her face, and threw the note back at Todd. It bounced from his nose to his desk.

"Young lady! What is your name?" called Mr. Bunn. "Please stand up!"

Skye froze in her seat at the sound of Mr.

Bunn's voice. Then she stood, very slowly, by the side of her desk. She felt as if her stomach had just fallen down into her shoes.

"Young lady, what is your name?" asked Mr. Bunn sternly.

"It's Skye Johnson," said Skye.

"Were you allowed to toss notes around in your old school?" asked Mr. Bunn.

"No, sir," said Skye. "But I was just . . . "

"I don't want to hear any excuses," said Mr. Bunn. "I have a special way of handling cases like this. Private notes are made public in this class," he said. "Would you please retrieve the note and read it out loud to the class. We would all like to know the important message that you had for the young man behind you."

Skye began to protest. "But I didn't . . . "

"Young lady, not another word. Just read the note," said Mr. Bunn. He held a piece of chalk in one hand and glared at Skye.

Skye's heart pounded as she walked back to Todd Kennedy's desk. She picked up the piece of paper from his desk and unfolded it.

"Please come to the front of the class," said Mr. Bunn.

"Oh, I wish that floors had mouths," Skye said to herself. She wished that *this* floor would open its mouth and swallow her. She wished that she would suddenly faint, and fall down onto the floor, and not move until everybody had left the room. But floors don't have mouths, and Skye's legs carried her to the front of the classroom.

"Please read the note to us," said Mr. Bunn. "You must have had a very important message for your friend. Let us hear it."

Skye felt tears rise to her eyes. She opened the note and read in a high voice, "I know you think I'm a jerk, but I like you anyway. Can I call you tonight?"

Laughter erupted from around the room. Marcia Glanders stared at Skye, and Todd Kennedy grinned. He called to the front of the room, "You can call me if you want to, Skye. I don't think you're such a jerk." He laughed and the rest of the class joined in. That is, everyone laughed except Mr. Bunn.

Mr. Bunn looked down at Skye and said, "From now on, young lady, you must keep your messages to yourself. I will not tolerate the throwing of notes in my class. Now, please take your seat."

Skye walked back to her desk. She felt like a puppy who had just been smacked with a newspaper. It's not fair! Skye thought. Mr. Bunn wouldn't even listen to me. Oh, that Todd Kennedy! All he ever does is get people in trouble. Skye sat down at her desk and stared straight ahead. She could feel people from around the class staring at her. Every once in a while she heard a little snort of laughter. "Oh, what a great way to begin a new school year!" she moaned to herself. "Now everyone will think that I have a crush on that nerd with the snotty handkerchief in his pocket. Gross!"

Skye sighed, and looked down at her notebook. She picked up her pen and began to write, "It's got to get better. It can't get worse. It's got to get better. It's got to get better. It's got to get . . ." The bell rang and Skye rushed out into the hall looking for her next class.

\* \* \* \* \*

Skye sat through math, science, and home-ec classes without saying a word. She tried not to blink her eyes or scratch her nose. It seems like you can get into trouble in this school for just about everything, she thought. Skye remembered all of the awful stories that Bill had told her. Maybe they were true, after all. Skye's hand shook as she thought about being forced by an eighth grader to lick water off of the floor. Actually, that wouldn't be as bad as having to read in front of a whole classroom a note that she hadn't written. So far, the teachers here were meaner than the students. It seemed like the older kids just ignored the sixth graders.

The bell rang at twelve-fifteen. Skye looked around for the cafeteria. She didn't know who she was going to sit with because Lizzie's lunch hour was earlier in the day. Skye followed a group of kids. It seemed so weird because no one was talking in the halls. At Duncan Elementary you could barely hear yourself think in the halls. All the kids laughed and shouted. But here it was different. It was a little like the nightmare that Skye had had the night before, where no one made a sound and Skye's shoes slapped against the floor. Skye listened to her shoes to see if they were making the same loud noises that they had made in her dream. But they weren't. The sounds of her steps were covered by the sounds of all the other shoes walking around her.

Skye found the cafeteria and walked in. She looked around for someone to sit with, but she only recognized one person. That person had a gray-looking handkerchief sticking out of his shirt pocket. Skye took her lunch tray and sat at the end of a long table by herself. At the other end sat a group of people who laughed and chattered together. Skye poked a fork into her creamed corn, thinking that it looked like something she saw the pigs eat on her grandmother's farm.

Skye nibbled on her roll and gazed around the lunchroom at the older kids. They were sitting in groups and they looked like they were having a good time. They even looked as if they liked being here. They probably know everyone, she thought, and they have lots of friends. They probably feel tough because they have some new sixth graders to pick on.

Skye checked her schedule. Next she had study hall until one-thirty. Then at one-thirty came gym class where she would get to see Lizzie again. Then, at two-thirty Skye had English. Thank goodness, Lizzie was in that class, too.

The bell rang and Skye returned her tray with most of its food still on it. Then she walked to the auditorium where her study hall was. The time went quickly and after study hall, Skye hurried to her locker for her gym bag. On her way there she saw a hall monitor give three boys and a girl pink slips for talking in the hall.

"Hi, Skye," came Nel's voice. "Do you have gym now?"

Skye widened her eyes, but didn't say a word. She'd already been in enough trouble for her first day at school. She didn't want to top it off with a pink slip. Skye nodded at Nel and pointed toward the gym. Nel understood, and with her gym bag tucked under her arm, she walked with Skye to the girls' dressing room.

It was a relief to open the door to the dressing room and walk in. At last, it was okay to talk. Girls on benches with their gym bags beside them chattered and giggled. A slender woman, wearing a white T-shirt and shorts, walked into the center of the room. She said, "Girls! May I have your attention, please. I'm Ms. Frazer. Today, we're going to play basketball. So, get into your gym clothes and come out into the gym."

Girls started pulling off shoes, hose, and sweaters. Skye stood frozen beside Nel and Lizzie as she watched the other girls around her undressing. "What's the matter?" asked Lizzie. She looked at Skye curiously. Skye didn't say a word. Lizzie followed Skye's gaze to where Marcia Glanders stood in blue bikini underwear and a blue lace bra. "Oh, I get it," said Lizzie. "You're wearing an undershirt."

"Sh-sh-sh!" hissed Skye. She pulled her sweater off over her head. Then she pulled her gym T-shirt over her blouse and undressed under the T-shirt as fast as she could. "Stand right there," Skye whispered to Lizzie. "And you stand right there, Nel. You guys can be a wall around me."

"You have to talk to your mother," said Lizzie. "This is getting ridiculous."

"Tell me about it," sighed Skye. "You don't think I *like* being a secret undershirt person, do you?"

"Come on. Let's go," said Nel. "Everyone else is already out in the gym."

Skye had played basketball with Bill before, so she was better than most of the other girls. She watched Marcia Glanders and saw that she was good at shooting baskets. Marcia wasn't very fast, but she moved gracefully. Once again, Skye wondered how good Marcia was at tennis.

At the end of class, Ms. Frazer said, "You did a fine job today girls. I can tell that some of you are going to be first-class basketball players. There's not much time left, so you'd better hurry back to the dressing room and shower up."

The girls moved in a group back to the locker room. Skye looked around and saw a large shower room beside the lockers. It had ten shower nozzles along one wall. The other girls looked into the shower room and began to whisper to each other. "Are you going to take all your clothes off? Are you going to take a shower?"

"Forget it," said Skye. "I'm not taking all of my clothes off."

"Me neither," said Lizzie.

"You have to draw the line somewhere," said Nel. "I'll do lots of weird things, but walking around naked isn't one of them."

Skye looked around to see what the other girls were doing. A few of them took their clothes off and walked into the showers. Skye had to admire them for being so brave. But right now, she belonged to the larger group of girls who chose to spray their armpits with an extra dose of deodorant, and then pull on their clothes.

Skye arranged Nel and Lizzie into an undershirt-protector wall, then she quickly pulled on her school clothes. As she dressed, she peeped enviously over at Marcia Glanders and her beautiful blue bra. As far as Skye could see, she was the *only* one in the whole gym class who didn't have a bra. Skye looked down at her sweater-covered chest and had to admit to herself that there wasn't much there to put into a bra. But that wasn't the point. The point is that without a bra, she thought, I'm different from everyone else. Without a bra I'm still a little girl, and I might as well be back in Duncan Elementary.

The bell rang and Skye hurried back to her locker to get her English book. It seemed weird to start hurrying every time she heard a bell between classes. Skye felt a little bit like a circus animal who was trained to jump through hoops at the sound of a cracking whip. Only for Skye it wasn't a whip. It was the sound of a bell that told her to rush from class to class.

Skye sat beside Lizzie in English class moments before the bell rang. "Hello, class. I'm Mrs. Perkins," said a woman in a yellow dress. "This is your last class of the day and I hope you're not too tired to do a little writing. For the rest of the class time I want each of you to write a few paragraphs about what your first day in the sixth grade has been like. The title should be *My First Day at Duncan Middle School.* All right? Are there any questions?"

Everyone in the class put their pen to paper and began writing. Skye looked around at all the students. She raised her hand.

"Yes? Do you have a question?" asked Mrs. Perkins. The other students quit writing and looked curiously at Skye.

"Are we being graded on this?" asked Skye.

Mrs. Perkins smiled. "No, you're not. Feel free to write whatever you want to write. There won't be a grade on this."

"Good," Skye muttered under her breath. She picked up her pen and began to write:

*My First Day at Duncan Middle School*

I had a nightmare the other night about my first day in sixth grade. But it turns out that my first day in this school was even worse than my nightmare. First of all, I can't believe how many rules there are. It seems like you can't even scratch an itch without someone giving you a pink slip.

Todd Kennedy got me into a lot of trouble in homeroom. It wasn't my fault, but Mr. Bunn wouldn't listen to me.

My gym class was really embarrassing, but I don't even want to talk about that.

The food in the lunchroom was crummy, but at least no one made me clean my plate like my brother, Bill, said they would. I hate creamed corn.

I hope this school gets better, because I think that if it doesn't I might go crazy.

Thank goodness for my best friend Lizzie.

Skye Johnson

# SIX

"DAD, it was awful," moaned Skye. "I don't usually like to complain, but sixth grade is really the pits. I can't believe Mr. Bunn blamed me for a note I didn't write. I tried to tell him."

Mr. Johnson sat in his favorite armchair with a book in his lap. He reached out and patted Skye's hand. "It sounds like you had a pretty lousy day," he said. "Why didn't you just tell Mr. Bunn that Todd wrote the note?"

"Dad, that's what I just said." Skye rolled her eyeballs back into her head. She thought, Sometimes when I talk to my dad I feel like he's from the moon or something. Why can't he understand me?

"I tried to tell Mr. Bunn, but he wouldn't let me," explained Skye. "I was totally embarrassed."

"It should be better tomorrow," said Mrs.

Johnson, walking into the room. She sat beside Skye on the couch and put her arm around her. Skye felt like pushing her mother's arm away even though it felt good to be hugged. It was nice to know that her mother cared.

"Mom, it might be worse tomorrow," said Skye. "I don't know if I can stand another day like today. I don't know which was worse, reading a note I didn't write in front of the class, or eating my lunch alone. It seems like I spent the whole day being embarrassed."

"What's the matter, Squirt?" asked Bill, dribbling an imaginary basketball into the room.

"I had a rotten day today," said Skye. "I don't think I'm going to like sixth grade."

"Come on, Skye," said Bill. "I'll bet you're just down because you're the only girl in the whole school who's not wearing a bra." Bill quit dribbling the imaginary ball, and began to laugh. "Don't feel bad," he said. "I have an old ace-bandage you can use. Just wrap it around your chest."

"Bill, I hate you!" yelled Skye.

"Young man, go to your room," said Mr. Johnson.

"But Dad," said Bill, "I was just kidding. I didn't mean to upset her. It was just a joke.

Sorry, Skye." Bill looked at his sister with concern. "I didn't know you took the bra business so seriously."

The tears that Skye had held back all day began to flow. Her shoulders shook as she began to cry.

"What's the matter, honey?" asked her mother.

"Really, Skye," exclaimed Bill. "Don't worry about it. Sixth grade will get better."

"Oh, Mom," sobbed Skye. "That's not it. It's just too embarrassing to talk about." She sniffed and wiped her nose on her arm.

"Now, Skye," said Mr. Johnson. "I hope we're the kind of parents that you can talk to. I know I've always tried to talk to you about things on your mind. You know you can talk to your mother and me about anything. Come on, now." He smiled invitingly at Skye. "You can tell us. What's on your mind?"

Skye hid her face behind her hands. "I want a bra," she mumbled.

"What's that?" asked her father. "You want your mom?"

"I'm right here, Skye," said Mrs. Johnson.

"No, that's not what I said," moaned Skye. "I said that I want a bra. Everyone in the whole school has one except me—and the boys. I'm the only *girl* in the whole middle school who still wears undershirts. Even Lizzie has a bra and she's just as flat as I am. I'm a freak. I can't stand it anymore!" Another tear trickled down Skye's cheek and fell onto her shoe. Skye looked down at the spot that it made. She began to cry again. "And another thing is that my feet are too big," she sobbed. Through her tears she saw that her mother was smiling and that made the hurt ten times worse.

"Oh, I knew you'd laugh," she cried. Skye looked at Bill to see if he was laughing at her, too. But he wasn't. For once, he was quiet and looked as if he cared.

"I'm not laughing at you," Mrs. Johnson hurried to say. "I'm just smiling because I remember going through the very same thing when I was your age. It's okay, honey. We can run out to the store right now and buy you a bra, if you'd like. Marshall's should still be open. I know that they have a teen section there."

Skye's tears stopped and her brown eyes began to shine. "Really?" she asked. "I can get one tonight?"

"Sure," said Mr. Johnson. "You can run out right now and get a bra. I don't know if Marshall's sells smaller feet, though. I'm afraid you'll have to learn to live with your own."

He smiled, and Skye began to laugh.

"I'm really sorry I hurt your feelings earlier," said Bill. "I didn't know how important getting a bra was to you. I'll drive you to Marshall's if you want me to," offered Bill.

"No, thanks," said Skye in an embarrassed voice. "I think I'd rather go with Mom. Somehow I don't think you're much of an expert on buying bras." Skye grinned shyly. "I'm sorry I cried," she said, looking around at her family. "It's just that I've been feeling down lately. And I really don't think I'm going to like sixth grade. I feel like my teachers hate me already and I haven't even done anything."

"Well," said Mr. Johnson. "There's no need to apologize. Everybody cries now and then. And as for your teachers hating you . . . I doubt that they do. But if you behave in class and do your work, I'm sure they'll get to know you and like you."

"There's just one more thing," Skye said, looking at her mother and holding her breath at the same time. "Can I get a blue bra with lace on it?"

"Good heavens!" said Mrs. Johnson. "Have you been reading *Seventeen Magazine* again? I don't even think that I have a blue lace bra. What in the world gave you that idea?"

"There's this girl at school named Marcia Glanders," said Skye. "She's real cute and popular, and she plays tennis. I think she might even be some kind of tennis pro. Anyway, she has a blue lace bra."

"I think a plain white one will do for you," said Mrs. Johnson. "We can look at the blue ones though. Come on, get your jacket. Let's go to Marshall's."

Mrs. Johnson and Skye drove to the department store and went to the teen underwear section. Skye didn't get a blue bra. Instead, she got three white bras with stretchy straps. They weren't nearly as lacy as the bras that Skye had imagined in her mind. But, they were bras, and that's all that really mattered. Skye wore one of them home. It felt neat under her blouse. Skye thought, This is weird. I know I'm eleven years old in an undershirt or in a bra. But when I'm wearing a bra, I feel older. How cool!

"Is everything okay now?" asked Mr. Johnson with a wink when Skye returned home.

"Oh, Dad," said Skye. "Let's not talk about it, okay? I've had enough embarrassment for one day." Skye walked back to her bedroom. She had the paper bag with the other two bras in it and she wanted to go to her room to look at them. In the hall she met Bill on his way to the bathroom.

"Hey, Squirt," he said. "What's in the bag?"

"You know what it is," said Skye and hugged the bag to her chest. Bill smiled as he walked past her. He leaned over and grabbed the back of her bra with his thumb and snapped it against her back.

"Bill, you creep!" yelled Skye. She slapped his arm with the bag.

"Bill, leave your sister alone!" Mrs. Johnson's voice came from the living room.

"I didn't say a word," Bill called back to her. "Not a word." He grinned at Skye and walked into the bathroom, closing the door behind him.

"You know what your problem is?" asked Skye through the bathroom door.

"What's that?" asked Bill.

"You just don't have any class," said Skye. "You think just because you're older than me, you have to embarrass me all the time."

Skye heard the toilet flush. She didn't want to meet her brother in the hall. He will probably just snap the back of my bra again, she thought. Skye went to her bedroom wondering if all older brothers were as immature as hers was. Skye had always hoped that her brother would turn into the kind of boy who would bring his cute friends home from school with him. She wished that he was the kind of boy who would drive her to parties and school dances, but no such luck. Instead, it looked like she was stuck with the kind of brother who snapped bras and acted like a jerk.

There was a knock on Skye's door and she said, "Come in."

Bill opened the door, stepping inside. He said, "You know, Skye. I hate to admit it, but you're right. I shouldn't try to embarrass you. I keep forgetting that you're not a kid anymore. Remember when I used to put soda pop in your Betsy Wetsy doll, and you cried because you thought she had diarrhea?"

"Yeah, I remember," said Skye with a smile. "That used to make me mad."

"I know," said Bill. "Well, I guess I need to realize that you're not that little kid anymore. You're growing up. It must be pretty tough going to a new school, making new friends, and growing up all at the same time." He smiled encouragingly. "But don't worry about it. You'll get used to all the new kids and teachers. You'll do just fine. You'll do better than fine because you're my sister."

Skye smiled back at her brother. "Do you really think so?" she asked. "Thanks. I'm sorry

I got so mad at you earlier, Bill."

"That's okay," said Bill. "There's just one more thing I wanted to ask you."

"What's that?" Skye asked, looking at her brother with curiosity. Bill shoved his hands into his jeans pockets and said, "Would you mind cleaning out the inside of Emmie for me tomorrow? I have a hot date tomorrow with Chrissie Evans and I don't have time to clean the car myself. Could you help me out? I'd really appreciate it."

Skye thought for a moment, then said, "Sure. I'll do it."

"Thanks," said Bill. "You know, you're an okay sister." He left Skye's room, closing the door.

Skye wondered, Why am I being so nice? One minute ago I was mad at him, and now I've agreed to clean out his car. It's funny how Bill can talk me into anything.

Skye did her homework. Then she got her other bras out of the bag and tried them on in front of the mirror. She posed this way and that way, a side view, then a front view. Even if it wasn't blue lace, it looked pretty nice, she thought. Skye thought about the crazy evening at home that had started out with tears and angry words, and had ended with a trip to the bra section at Marshall's. She also thought about how family members can surprise you sometimes. Bill was being nice and her mother hadn't even batted an eye when Skye asked her for a bra. Here she had been embarrassed to ask her mom for a bra. She just knew that her mom wouldn't understand. But she did understand. Skye shook her head as she thought of all the worrying she had done for nothing.

Skye pulled her nightgown on over her head. She slept with her bra on that night.

In the morning when she got ready for school, Skye thought about gym class. Today, I won't need the undershirt wall. I won't need to arrange Nel and Lizzie around me so that no one else can see me, she thought happily.

Skye climbed onto the bus whistling a tune under her breath. "Hey there, little gal," said the bus driver.

"Hi," said Skye. She wasn't going to let this bus driver get her down . . . not today. Finally, she wasn't different from any other girl in the school. Skye walked to the back of the bus where she sat next to a window. The bus drove on and stopped on the next street.

"Hey, Skye," said Todd, stopping next to her seat. "Mind if I sit down?"

"Yes, I do," said Skye, looking up at the boy with the crumpled handkerchief sticking out of his pocket. "Go sit somewhere else."

"I'll pretend you didn't say that," said Todd, sliding into the empty seat next to Skye. Skye made a face and sighed. The bus pulled out into the street and rumbled on, taking Skye to her second day at Duncan Middle School. When Lizzie got on the bus, she saw Todd sitting beside Skye and took a front seat.

Lizzie met Skye at her locker before homeroom. "Where were you last night?" she asked. "I called about a million times. Bill kept answering the phone and saying that you'd moved to Texas to become a cowgirl."

"What a jerk," sighed Skye. "I was at Marshall's with my mom." Skye smiled broadly. "You'll never guess what I got," she said excitedly.

"A bra? Great!" said Lizzie.

"Sh-sh," hissed Skye. "You don't have to tell the whole world."

"Sorry," said Lizzie. Her voice sunk to a whisper. "Congratulations," she said. "Welcome to the bra club."

"Excuse me, but you two girls shouldn't be talking. It's against the rules," said a hall monitor. "I'm going to have to give both of you a pink slip. What are your names?"

Skye felt her face turning pink. "Skye Johnson," she said.

Lizzie frowned. "I'm Lizzie Stutz," she said. "Come on. Give us a break."

"I'll have to give you a green slip if you argue with me," said the girl.

"Sorry. She didn't mean anything," said Skye. "Give us the slips."

"Okay. Here you go." The girl handed a pink slip to Skye and Lizzie. "Now, don't talk in the halls anymore. We're pretty strict about that here." The girl walked off into the crowd.

"Can you believe that?" asked Lizzie.

"Sh-sh!" whispered Skye.

"It looks like you two got caught," whispered Kurt Freeman. He smiled and Skye looked back at the blond-haired seventh grader who had just walked up. "You'll learn how to get around the rules after a while," he said. Then he disappeared through a classroom door.

"Wow! Kurt Freeman talked to us!" whispered Lizzie. "Well, see you later." She climbed the stairs to her homeroom, while Skye went downstairs to hers. She walked into the room and saw Marcia Glanders sitting in the first row. Today, she had on a bright red blouse with a black leather skirt. She was wearing hose again and a silver bracelet dangled from her wrist. Suddenly, Skye felt clunky. She felt as if she were wearing shoe boxes for shoes, and she felt like her plain wool skirt was woven out of dog hair. This day started out so great, thought Skye, and already it is going downhill. Skye remembered back to the early morning when she was putting on her school clothes and new bra. A smile came back to her face and she sat down at her desk.

"Good morning, class," said Mr. Bunn. "Today we're going to work out a permanent seating arrangement. I'll begin by calling roll."

A crumpled piece of paper came flying through the air and fell onto Skye's desk. She gasped as she realized that Todd Kennedy was sending another airmail note. Skye took the paper ball in her hand and quietly dropped it on the floor beside her desk. For once she was grateful for her sturdy shoes as she felt the note under her foot. She squashed the paper with her shoe and kicked it backward down the aisle.

"Skye Johnson?" came Mr. Bunn's voice from the front of the room.

"I didn't do anything! Honest, I didn't!" said Skye.

"I'm just calling the roll," said Mr. Bunn.

"Oh-h-h," stammered Skye. "I'm here."

Skye looked at the clock on the wall. She opened her notebook and saw the page that she'd written on yesterday in homeroom. It said, "It's got to get better. It can't get worse. It's got to get better. It's got to get better. It's got to get . . . "

Skye wrote underneath it, "It's getting worse."

# SEVEN

"BUT Lizzie, we've been in school for two weeks now and I still haven't met any of the seventh or eighth graders," Skye said. She lay on her bed with the telephone balanced on her stomach.

"We met that eighth-grade girl who gave us the pink slips," said Lizzie.

"That's not exactly what I call making a new friend," sighed Skye. "It just seems like the older kids won't even speak to us. What's so gross about sixth graders? I'm beginning to think we all smell like cow dung or something."

Lizzie laughed. "Give them time," she said. "Maybe once they get to know us, they'll like us."

"How are they going to get to know us if they won't even talk to us?" asked Skye. She thought for a moment, then she said, "You know, I just had a great idea. I've seen signs around school about a Harvest Dance. It's the first week in October. I'll bet if we went to that dance we could meet a lot of people."

"You mean we should go there without dates?" asked Lizzie.

"Sure," said Skye. "You, Amy, Nel, and I could all go together. Maybe Bill could drive us. If we get all dressed up and look really dynamite, maybe some of the older guys will notice us."

"It's worth a try," said Lizzie. "I'll call Amy and Nel and see what they think about it. Do you think your parents will let you go?"

"Are you kidding?" asked Skye. "Parents *live* for that kind of stuff. As soon as I tell my mom about it she'll start going crazy about what I should wear and how I should fix my hair."

"Great!" said Lizzie. "It sounds like fun. Hmmmm. Maybe Kurt Freeman will be there."

"I thought you didn't care about boys," said Skye teasingly.

"Well, you know, they're kind of growing on me. At least Kurt doesn't seem as silly as some of the others," Lizzie confessed. "He seems like the kind of guy that you could play basketball with. I don't think I'd have to act dumb and giggly around Kurt."

"Who says you have to act dumb and giggly around boys?" asked Skye.

"I don't know," said Lizzie. "It just seems like some of the older girls act that way."

"Probably it's because they have their periods," said Skye. "Remember that pact we made last summer, that we aren't going to turn weird when we start our periods?"

"Yeah."

"Well, I'm keeping my end of the deal," said Skye.

"You haven't started your period yet, have you?" asked Lizzie.

"No. But I still promise that I won't be weird around boys, whether I have my period or not."

"You know," said Lizzie. "Since Kurt lives just down the street from me, I might be able to walk to the bus with him sometime. That would be a good chance to get to know him better. Then I can make my move at the Harvest Dance."

A pounding came from outside Skye's bedroom door. "Get off the phone!" Bill yelled. "I need to call Alex. You'd better watch out or that thing will get stuck to your ear."

"Go away, creep!" yelled Skye. "I have to go," she said to Lizzie. "The jerk needs to use the phone. Call me later, okay? And be sure to call Nel and Amy about the dance. I'm so excited! I can't wait!"

"Hurry up in there!" yelled Bill.

"Bye," said Skye, and she hung up the phone.

* * * * *

"Oh, honey, that's wonderful!" said Mrs. Johnson. "I'm sure you'll meet lots of new friends at the Harvest Dance. Now, what are you going to wear? How about that cute lilac dress with the pearl buttons? We could curl your hair, too, if you'd like."

"Pass the ketchup, please," said Skye. She looked at her family gathered around the dinner table. "Sure, Mom. The lilac dress would be nice. But what shoes am I going to wear?"

"We'll find something, honey," said Mrs. Johnson. "Maybe you should get a new pair."

"Maybe you could get new feet while you're at it," said Bill. "Pass the potatoes, please."

Skye started to say something angrily back to Bill, but she changed her mind. Instead, she smiled sweetly and said, "Bill, dear brother, would you please drive me, Amy, Nel, and Lizzie to the dance?"

"Sorry," said Bill. "I may have a date that night. You never can tell."

Skye thought for a moment. "I'll shine up Emmie's hubcaps for you if you drive us," she offered.

"Emmie doesn't have hubcaps," said Bill.

"I'll set the table for a week," said Skye.

"You have a deal," said Bill. He shook hands with Skye over a bowl of mashed potatoes.

\* \* \* \* \*

Skye spent the next two weeks trading makeup with Nel, Amy, and Lizzie. She sat in front of her mirror and tried new hair styles. Some afternoons Lizzie came home with her after school. Skye and Lizzie put on records and practiced doing the latest dance steps in Skye's bedroom.

One afternoon, Bill stuck his head in the door and said, "What are you two up to? Are you still trying to learn to dance?" He grinned and then continued, "You might as well give it up. That's impossible."

Skye threw a pillow at him. "I've set the table all week," she said. "Remember, you promised to drive us."

"Don't worry, Squirt," said Bill. "Emmie

and I will take you to the dance in style. We'll give you a night you'll never forget. I promise." He smiled and winked, then left the room.

"I don't trust your brother," said Lizzie.

"He'll be okay," said Skye. "He promised he'd take us. Wow! I can't wait! Just think of all the new guys we're going to meet!"

"Yeah," said Lizzie. "And I'm finally going to get to dance with Kurt Freeman."

"I wonder who I'll dance with?" mused Skye. "I sure hope he's cute. Who knows? Maybe I'll find a boyfriend at the Harvest Dance."

# EIGHT

"HOW do I look?" asked Skye. She twirled across the room in her lilac-colored dress.

"You look great!" said Mr. Johnson.

"You look like you just stepped out of a magazine," said Mrs. Johnson.

"Not bad for a sixth grader," said Bill. "Are you ready to go? Emmie's warming up out in the driveway."

"Does this lip gloss look okay with this dress?" asked Skye. "Did I put on too much?"

"No, honey." Mrs. Johnson smiled. "Your lip gloss looks fine."

"Come on," said Bill. "Let's get going."

"My slip isn't showing, is it?" asked Skye anxiously.

"No. And your bra's not falling off either," said Bill. "Come on. Let's go."

"Have a good time, dear," said Mrs.

Johnson. "Don't forget. Bill will pick you girls up at ten-thirty."

"Right. Let's go," Bill said hurriedly. He opened the front door and stepped out into the cold October night. Emmie sat trembling and puffing in the driveway. "She's good and warm," called Bill, patting Emmie's hood. He opened the door and scooted into the driver's seat.

Skye pulled on a coat over her dress. She made her I'm-afraid-I'm-going-to-die face and said good-bye to her parents. "You'll do fine," said Mr. Johnson. "Don't worry. You'll be the hit of the dance."

Bill honked Emmie's horn. "Come on, Skye!" he called.

Skye climbed into the seat beside Bill. He backed Emmie out of the driveway and headed for Lizzie's house. Bill honked the horn as he pulled into the Stutz' driveway. Lizzie came running out. She scooted into the backseat with a rustling of nylon slip and hose.

"I like your hair," said Skye. "What did you do to it?"

"I washed it," said Lizzie.

"Well, it looks real good," laughed Skye. She turned to Bill, saying, "We have to pick up Nel and Amy."

"I know. I know. Keep your shirt on," said

Bill. He backed the car onto the street. Suddenly Emmie began to cough and splutter. A puff of smoke burst out from under the car's hood. "Uh oh," said Bill, with a frown. "This looks serious."

"Hey, it's beginning to shake back here," said Lizzie worriedly.

"It's shaking up here, too," said Skye. "Oh, great! Bill, is this car going to fall apart before we get to the dance?"

"Have faith," said Bill. "Emmie hasn't let me down yet. Have you, girl?" He patted the steering wheel. A shower of sparks flew out from under the hood. "She's just flirting with me," said Bill. "She just needs a little love. That's all."

"And I thought I was hard up," muttered Skye. "At least I'm not having a relationship with a car."

"I'm not kidding," said Bill. "Emmie is very sensitive. She needs to know that you guys love her."

"Is this for real?" asked Lizzie. "Are you serious?"

A violent shudder ran from the front wheels to the back.

"Darn right, I'm serious!" exclaimed Bill. "Emmie's not going to move another inch unless you guys tell her that you're sorry for all the bad things you've said about her. Tell her she's a good ol' car."

"Bill, I'm going to kill you," said Skye, trying to control her temper. "I spent all day getting ready for this dance. Can't you do something about this crummy car?"

Another shower of sparks flew out from under the hood. "Yikes!" yelled Lizzie. "We're not going to burn up, are we?"

"Not if you tell Emmie that she's a good ol' car," said Bill.

"Okay. Okay," said Lizzie. "I'll say it. You're a good ol' car, Emmie. You're a great ol' car, and we'd really appreciate it if you'd pick up Nel and Amy and take us to the dance. Now, you say it, Skye. Tell Emmie she's a good ol' car."

"Forget it," said Skye. "I might only be eleven years old, but I know when my leg's being pulled. Bill, come on. Make this car run right. I know you're just doing this to be mean. I'm not kidding. This isn't funny."

Bill looked into Skye's determined eyes. "Okay," he said. "I'll tell her for you." He patted the dashboard. "Come on, Emmie ol' girl," he said. "Skye likes you, too, even though she won't admit it. Let's go to the dance, okay? You can do it." Bill reached under the dashboard and jiggled some wires.

With a rumble and groan, the blue and yellow car lurched forward. Bill drove to Amy's and Nel's homes. Later, the four girls giggled and whispered as Bill headed the car toward the middle school. As the car pulled into the parking lot, Skye turned to her friends and asked, "Are you sure I look all right?"

Nel asked, "Did I wear too much eyeshadow?"

"I just know that I'm going to sweat in this stupid dress," said Lizzie. "I know I should've worn that dark green one. I'll have to keep my arms down all night."

"Come on, you guys. Let's go in," said Amy. "We can hide in the bathroom for a while." The girls opened the doors and climbed out.

"Just a minute, Skye," Bill said, grabbing her arm. Skye chewed on her bottom lip nervously.

"What is it?" she asked, glaring at Bill.

"I just wanted to tell you to have a good time," he said. He smiled.

"What's the catch?" asked Skye.

"There's no catch," said Bill sheepishly. "I didn't mean to scare you about the car not working. I'm sorry I gave you such a hard time. Really, I am. I guess I'm a little rough on you sometimes. You know, for a kid sister, you're okay."

Skye's mouth softened into a smile. She stared into her big brother's eyes. "Thanks," she said.

"Oh. And there's another thing," said Bill. "You really do look dynamite tonight. Bye. I'll pick you guys up at ten-thirty."

"Come on, Skye," called Lizzie. "It's cold out here."

"Bye," said Skye. "Wish me luck."

"Luck," said Bill. Skye climbed out of the front seat and closed the door. With a roar of the engine, Bill raced Emmie off into the dark night.

"My brother amazes me sometimes," said Skye, turning to her friends. "He can be so mean, and then he can be so nice. It's weird. Maybe his brain's getting hard."

"My toes are getting hard out here in the cold in these stupid shoes," said Lizzie. "Let's go in."

The four girls climbed the steps to the school's front doors. They could hear music coming from the gymnasium. As they walked down the corridor, the music became louder. "I feel like I'm walking into the middle of a circus ring," said Amy. "You sure you guys don't want to go hide in the bathroom for a while?"

"No way," said Skye. "I've been waiting two

weeks for this thing. I came here to dance!"
Skye paused at the gymnasium door. She
looked around at the paper streamers that
looped across the ceiling. The bleachers were
filled with groups of students dressed in their
very best party clothes. Some of the overhead
lights had colored bulbs. The room was dark
and looked something like a dream. A slow
song played from a record player and couples
danced together in the middle of a shiny floor.

Skye looked around at the boys in dark suits
who stood nervously in little clusters. Most of
them looked like they'd rather be wearing
jeans and T-shirts. But Skye thought to
herself that they looked cute. She wondered if
hidden somewhere in this group was a boy
whom she had never met. Perhaps before the
night was over, she would be dancing with a
new boy who liked to play tennis and who
hated liver. Maybe he would look at her with a
smile on his face that said, "I like you. You're
pretty." Maybe he would be a seventh grader,
and it was possible that he might even be an
eighth grader. It was hard to guess. The night
stretched ahead with many possibilities.

"Hey, jerk. You want to dance?" Skye
cringed as she recognized the voice. Skye
whirled around to see Todd Kennedy standing
beside her. He was wearing a rumpled dark

green suit with a pink shirt. A handkerchief bulged from his breast pocket.

* * * * *

Skye stood in front of the bathroom mirror trading lip gloss with Amy, Nel, and Lizzie. "Help me," pleaded Skye. "I can't escape from Todd. I've danced with him three times in a row. Everyone's going to think we're married."

"Maybe he loves you," suggested Nel. She smacked her lips together in front of the mirror.

"Don't make me barf," said Skye. "I'm serious. I can't get rid of him. Would one of you guys *please* dance with him?"

"Forget it," said Amy. "I have my eye on a seventh grader named Dan. He's in my study hall."

"Count me out," said Lizzie. "I have my eye on Kurt Freeman. I'm trying to send him some brain-waves so he'll ask me to dance. I'm going to wait for two more songs to play, then if he hasn't asked me I'm going to ask him."

"P-l-e-a-s-e!" moaned Skye. "Todd's ruining my night. Maybe if one of you guys asks him to dance, he'll get up the courage to ask other girls to dance. He's just asking me because he thinks I'm the only one who'll dance with him. Please ask him."

"Okay. I'll do it," said Lizzie. "Anything for a friend. But just once, okay?"

Skye breathed a sigh of relief. "Oh, thanks, Lizzie," she said. "You're a true friend. I'll never forget this. I promise."

"You owe me one," said Lizzie, smiling. The girls put their lip gloss back into their purses and straightened their dresses. They returned to the gym where Lizzie whispered, "Okay. Here goes nothing."

Lizzie gritted her teeth and walked up to Todd. From the corner of her eye, Skye watched Lizzie ask him to dance. Todd grinned and nodded. He took Lizzie's hand and began to count out loud, "One-two-three. One-two-three." Lizzie rocked back and forth with him in time to the music. Skye smiled as she thought about what a good friend Lizzie was. She walked over to the bleachers and sat down.

"Would you like to dance?"

Skye looked up. She was too shocked to say a word and just stared back at the blond boy who stood in front of her. "I'm sorry," he said. "You don't know me. I should have introduced myself first. I'm Kurt Freeman. Now, would you like to dance?"

"Sure," said Skye. She stood up with her

lilac dress shining under the soft lights. Kurt took her hand and led her out onto the dance floor. He put his other hand gently against Skye's back. It was easy to follow Kurt as he glided over the floor. It felt wonderful to be whirling around in the arms of a cute seventh-grade boy. Skye relaxed her shoulders as she and Kurt moved smoothly together in time to the music.

Skye peeped over Kurt's shoulder and became aware of a set of eyes staring at her. She peered into the dark room and saw that the eyes belonged to Lizzie. Lizzie said something. Skye couldn't hear her words because of the music that filled the room. But she read her lips. Lizzie was saying, "Thanks a lot, friend. Thanks a lot."

Skye didn't know what to do. Her best friend in the world was doing her a favor by dancing with Todd. And she, Skye Johnson, was letting her friend down by dancing with the boy of Lizzie's dreams. Skye realized that she was dancing with the only boy in the whole school that Lizzie liked. Suddenly, she felt guilty, but there was another feeling that she had, too. She felt really good dancing with Kurt. He seemed nice. He was cute, and after all, Lizzie really didn't have any claim on him. It's not as if he's her boyfriend or anything like that, Skye thought. He's never asked Lizzie out on a date. Lizzie just has a crush on him. That's *her* problem. Lizzie will just have to deal with it, thought Skye.

"I've noticed you in the halls," said Kurt. "I know you're a sixth grader. How do you like middle school so far?"

"I love it," said Skye. "I've met a lot of nice people." It was a white lie. But suddenly, looking into Kurt's face, it became the truth. Skye looked shyly at Kurt, thinking that she'd finally met someone older than herself . . . someone who was cute and nice. He seemed like the kind of boy who liked himself and liked other people, too.

The song ended, and Kurt said, "How about another dance?"

"Sure," said Skye. "I'd love to."

Skye's brown eyes sparkled back at Kurt's blue ones. Then Skye looked over at the bleachers where Lizzie, Nel, and Amy stood talking to each other. All three of them looked angry. Skye watched them as they walked toward the girls' bathroom. "I wonder what's wrong with them?" she asked herself.

# *NINE*

SKYE lay on her bed and stared at the ceiling. She thought about how her life had changed since the Harvest Dance. That was three days ago. In that time Lizzie hadn't called her on the phone even once. Skye had called Lizzie twice, but each time Lizzie had said that she was busy and couldn't talk. Also, Lizzie and Nel dressed in a different part of the locker room during gym class. Lizzie wasn't speaking to Skye in English class, either.

Skye asked Amy about it. She stopped Amy one day in the hall at school. Skye said, "Come on, Amy. Tell me what's going on. Why are you guys ignoring me? Is it because I danced with Kurt at the Harvest Dance?"

"Lizzie says that you did it on purpose, because you knew that she liked Kurt," said Amy. "That was a rotten thing to do to your best friend, wasn't it?"

"I didn't *know* Kurt was going to ask me to dance," said Skye. "He just did, that's all. I don't see why I should feel bad about it."

"Well, maybe you should feel bad because you've just lost your three closest friends," said Amy. She tucked her books under her arm and strode down the hall.

"Am I dreaming?" Skye asked herself. "I can't believe my friends are acting this way." The rest of the week passed by and Skye spent the time alone. Her friends didn't call her at home or visit with her by her locker at school. Even Todd Kennedy wasn't following her around anymore. Skye saw him on the bus every morning and afternoon. He always sat up by the bus driver, and he always saved a seat for Lizzie. It was strange to suddenly have no friends.

Skye kept thinking about the whole situation. It doesn't seem fair, she thought. It's as if my friends have turned against me for no reason. Amy and Nel are on Lizzie's side. Probably Lizzie has told them to ignore me. That is just like Lizzie, Skye thought. Lizzie is so sure of herself. She acts like she's an expert on everything. She's always telling me how to act, what to say, and what to think. At least, she used to.

Now, Lizzie wasn't telling Skye anything at all.

* * * * *

"What's the matter, honey?" asked Mrs. Johnson. "You've been upset ever since the Harvest Dance. Do you have a crush on someone?"

Skye was in the kitchen helping her mother with dinner. She explained the whole story to Mrs. Johnson. As she told her mother what had happened at the dance, Skye didn't feel sad. She felt angry. "I only danced with Kurt three times," said Skye. "Then he started asking Marcia Glanders to dance. But Lizzie, Nel, and Amy started ignoring me. I was stuck there practically alone until 10:30. It was awful. I didn't know anyone and I had to sit alone on the bleachers."

"It sounds like Lizzie's jealous of you," said Mrs. Johnson.

Skye looked up in shock. "Aw, Mom. I don't think so. Everyone likes Lizzie, and she's never shy or embarrassed like I am. She doesn't act like a nerd around boys, either. She really seems to have it together. Why would she be jealous of me?"

"There's never a good reason for why

someone is jealous," sighed Mrs. Johnson. "Usually, it's because they're feeling bad about themselves. Then they start thinking that someone else is better than they are. It's just silliness. But then, people can act pretty silly sometimes, can't they?"

"I guess so," said Skye. "But it seems like Lizzie could at least give me a break since I'm her best friend. She won't even talk to me about it. Neither will Amy or Nel."

"I don't know what to tell you," said Mrs. Johnson, wiping her hands on her apron. "Maybe you could write Lizzie a letter. Tell her how you feel. Tell her that you're sorry that she feels this way."

"But I'm NOT sorry," said Skye. "I haven't done anything wrong! Lizzie should call me and tell *me* that *she's* sorry for acting like such a jerk."

"Hi, Squirt," said Bill, walking into the kitchen. He opened the refrigerator door and pulled out a carton of milk. "I've noticed you haven't been getting too many phone calls lately," he said. "Lizzie hasn't been over either. What's the matter? Do you have some kind of disease?"

"Please, Bill," moaned Skye. "I don't feel like fighting with you right now. I'm fighting with everyone else. I was hoping that at least my family could be nice to me."

"Oh," said Bill. "This sounds serious. What's the problem?"

"Lizzie, Amy, and Nel aren't speaking to me," said Skye. "I'm bored and I don't have any friends to goof around with."

"Whenever I'm bored, I do something physical," said Bill. "Like, I mow the lawn or go swimming or play tennis."

"It's winter," said Skye. "Those are summer things."

"Not if you join a team at school," said Bill with a wink.

"The middle school doesn't have a swimming pool," said Skye.

"Then why don't you try out for the tennis team?" asked Bill. "I was a member when I was in middle school. My coach was Ms. Frazer and she's really good. See? Your problems are solved. It's as easy as one-two-three." Bill snapped his fingers and left the kitchen.

Skye looked at her mother. "I hate to admit it, but I think Bill's right," she said. "Maybe I should try out for the tennis team."

"It couldn't hurt," said Mrs. Johnson. "And it might take your mind off of Lizzie."

Skye's face brightened. "Okay. I'll do it!" she said.

The next day after gym class, Skye spoke with Ms. Frazer.

"I'm sorry," said Ms. Frazer. "Tryouts for the tennis team were two weeks ago."

Skye's mouth dropped into a worried frown. "I didn't know when tryouts were," she admitted. "Have you had a lot of practices yet?"

"No," said Ms. Frazer. "We have our first team practice today after school." She thought for a moment. "You know, Skye, you could come to the gym after school today and meet the rest of the tennis team. Maybe we could watch you play and then have a vote on it. It's past the deadline for joining, but you seem to want to play so much, and we could use another person on the team."

"Oh, I really want to," said Skye. "It would mean a lot to me. I love tennis. My mom and brother both play with me in the summer."

"Okay," said Ms. Frazer. "We'll see you after school today in the gym."

Skye's next class was English. She sat beside Lizzie who stared straight ahead at the blackboard. It was hard for Skye not to talk to Lizzie because they had been best friends for so many years. But if Lizzie is going to keep acting like such a baby, thought Skye, then I'm not going to be the first one to give in. Lizzie would never be the first one to say that she was sorry, not for a million bucks. All this fuss over a boy . . . how silly!

After school, Skye almost ran down the halls to the girls' locker room. She changed into her gym clothes and hurried to the gym. A group of boys and girls stood in the middle of the floor, setting up nets and swinging their rackets. "Oh, no," Skye whispered to herself. "I don't know if I can stand it." There on the floor sat Marcia Glanders doing her stretching exercises. Her long slender legs ended in feet that pointed as gracefully as a ballerina's. Skye looked down at her own feet. They seemed huge in her white gym shoes.

"Hi, Skye. I didn't know you played tennis. Ms. Frazer says you're going to try out for the team." The voice sounded familiar. Skye's stomach did a somersault as she looked up into Kurt Freeman's face.

"Hi, Kurt," she said. "I didn't know that you played tennis, either." Skye tried to smile.

"Sure," he said. "It beats football. At least I'm not getting my brains bashed in," he laughed. "Have you met the other members of the team?"

"No," admitted Skye shyly.

"Come on," he said, taking Skye by the elbow. "I'll introduce you. This is Marcia. She and I have played tennis together for years. She's an old friend."

Marcia smiled and looked up from her exercising. "Hi," she said.

"Hi," said Skye. "We're in the same homeroom. I sit a few rows behind you."

"Oh, really?" said Marcia. She patted her shining red hair with the palm of her hand. "Oh! I remember. You're the girl who threw the note on the first day of class, aren't you?" Marcia began to laugh and Skye felt her face blushing.

"Well, that was kind of an accident," said Skye. "What *really* happened was . . . "

"Class!" yelled Ms. Frazer. "Quiet, please. Let's begin our practice. First of all, I'd like for all of you to meet Skye Johnson. She's in sixth grade and she'd like to join the tennis team."

"But tryouts were two weeks ago," said Marcia.

"Yes, but I thought we might bend the rules a little," admitted Ms. Frazer. "First we need to see how Skye plays. Any volunteers?"

"I will," said Marcia. She picked up her racket as she stood up. Then she gracefully walked out onto the gym floor. Skye felt her heart beat faster as she joined Marcia on the court and faced her from the other side of the net. "I'll serve first," said Marcia.

Skye held her breath as she realized that by serving, Marcia would have the advantage. Skye held her racket tightly and crouched. She knew that Ms. Frazer, Kurt Freeman, and the other tennis team members were standing on the sidelines, watching her. Marcia tossed the ball in the air and stretched her body as she served it over the net. The ball whizzed right by Skye as she swung her racket. She spun around and almost fell to the ground. There was no other sound in the gym except for the heavy breathing of Skye and Marcia as they faced each other. "15-Love," called Ms. Frazer.

Skye thought to herself, Oh, no! I'm in big trouble. I have to hit one back.

Marcia served the ball again, and this time Skye was able to return it. Marcia ran and hit the ball back over the net, but Skye was ready. She leaped into the air and slammed the ball back onto Marcia's court. Marcia's racket just missed it, and the score was even. "15-15," called Ms. Frazer.

Marcia won the next point. Skye felt droplets of sweat forming on her forehead. "30-15," called Ms. Frazer. Skye tried to pretend that she wasn't playing tennis with one of the cutest and most popular girls in the sixth grade. She tried to pretend that her brother, Bill, was on the other side of the net. Skye won the next point. She won the next one, too. "30-40," said Ms. Frazer. Skye looked at Marcia's face. Marcia's eyes concentrated on the ball. She took a deep breath and hit the ball to Skye. Skye returned it, but it bounced out of bounds and Marcia won the point. Marcia served again and Skye returned it. Marcia missed the ball.

"Game point," said Ms. Frazer. Skye felt a drop of sweat fall into her eye. She realized that she could win the game if she beat Marcia on this point.

Marcia served the ball. Skye ran to the corner of the court and hit the ball. Marcia ran toward the net, barely reaching it in time to hit the ball back to Skye. Skye swung her racket and the ball flew over the net. Marcia lunged for it, but the ball sped past her.

"You win," said Marcia.

"Good playing, girls," said Ms. Frazer. "You both did a good job."

"Thanks," said Skye. She wiped the perspiration from her forehead with the back of her hand. Then she walked toward the other team members on the sidelines.

Ms. Frazer faced the members and said, "We need to decide whether or not Skye should be on the tennis team. You just saw how she plays. Should we have the vote now or later?"

Marcia walked up and joined the group. She was still breathing heavily from the game. "Let's decide now," she said. "I vote that we let Skye join the team. She's really good! She'll make our team a lot stronger."

"I second it," said Kurt. "Let Skye join the team."

One by one, hands went up into the air. Everyone agreed.

"Great!" said Ms. Frazer. "Welcome to the team, Skye. We have practice every Thursday after school and on Saturday mornings. Okay, now. Let's practice. Everyone out onto the court. We'll start with a game of doubles."

The other team members began pairing off and walking out onto the court. Skye was embarrassed for a moment as she realized that she was the new person on the team and didn't have a partner.

"Want to play with me?" asked Marcia. She smiled a lovely smile at Skye. "I think we'd make a good team," she said.

"I do, too," said Skye. "You have a good backhand. Maybe you could help me with mine."

"Sure," said Marcia, "if you help me with my serves." She smiled again at Skye, and

Skye felt her insides turn warm as she realized that this was the beginning of a nice, new friendship. She smiled to herself as she thought about it.

Skye walked with Marcia onto the gym floor where they stood facing their opponents on the opposite court. Skye prepared to serve the ball. She held it in one hand. Then she held her racket in the other hand and stretched her arm back as far as it would go. R-i-i-i-i-i-ip! A sudden breeze blew under Skye's arm. Marcia began to laugh. Skye looked over her shoulder at the tear in the back of her blouse.

She sighed to herself and thought, That's just my luck! This is one of the greatest days of my life. I've just joined the tennis team. I've made a new friend. And now my shirt rips open in front of everyone. Oh, well. I guess I'd rather have a ripped shirt and a new friend, than a good shirt and no friends at all.

Skye grinned at Marcia and shrugged her shoulders. Then she faced her opponents and served the ball.

# TEN

FOR the next two weeks Skye practiced with the tennis team, getting to know Marcia and Kurt better. She spent the night at Marcia's house one Saturday night, and discovered that Marcia was more than pretty. She was nice, too. Skye also found out that Marcia was just as afraid to come to the middle school as she was. It seemed funny to Skye that a girl as cute as Marcia would be afraid of going to a new school.

It was nice to have a new friend, but Skye still felt as if something was wrong. She felt uncomfortable sitting beside Lizzie in English and not talking to her. It's awful, Skye thought, not having the phone ring all the time like it used to. Marcia doesn't like to talk on the phone like Lizzie does. New friends are great. But old friends are important, too. I miss Lizzie, she sighed to herself.

One Friday afternoon in English class Mrs. Perkins said, "Class! I'm going to hand back some old papers today. Do you remember your first day here at the middle school?" A groan rose from the classroom. Mrs. Perkins laughed. "Remember the page that you wrote for me about your first day? Well, I thought that since you've been in school for several months now, you might find these papers amusing. I'm going to pass them back to you. I think you'll find it interesting to see how you felt about coming to a new school at the beginning of the year."

Mrs. Perkins passed out the papers. Skye had to chuckle to herself when she read her own essay. Then she peeped out of the corner of her eye to see what Lizzie was doing. Lizzie sat quietly at her desk, reading her essay. Her eyes looked serious and her lips were turned down into a frown. Skye faced the front of the classroom as Mrs. Perkins began to explain the homework assignment.

A bell rang at the end of class. All the students jumped up from their desks and began to push toward the door. Skye gathered her books and let the others hurry past her. She glanced at Lizzie's desk. Lizzie had left the classroom with everyone else, not bothering to wait for Skye. A sheet of paper lay on Lizzie's desk. Skye picked up the paper and started to call Lizzie who was just disappearing into the hall. But then Skye remembered that she and Lizzie weren't speaking to each other, so she silently held the paper in her hand.

Skye took a quick glance at Lizzie's paper. She took a closer look as she recognized her name among the words written there. She began to read:

### My First Day at Duncan Middle School

It's weird coming to a new school because some of the kids here are real turkeys. In fact, there seem to be an awful lot of them in this school. Even the teachers are kind of weird. But I don't really mind it because I have one good friend with me. Her name is Skye. Skye's name makes me think of sunshine and blue skies, and moonlight in a dark sky. I'm glad that Skye is my friend, because if she wasn't, I probably couldn't stand being here! She'll always be my friend.

Lizzie Stutz

As Skye read Lizzie's paper, she felt the tears begin to rise to her eyes. They used to be such good friends, and now because of a stupid misunderstanding, they weren't even speaking to each other. All those years of friendship, Skye thought, are going down the drain because we're both just too stubborn to admit that we still love and care for each other. Skye wondered if Lizzie felt the same way that she did.

She grabbed her books and ran into the hall. It was crowded with students. "Lizzie! Lizzie!" Skye began to call.

Lizzie's voice called, "Here I am."

Skye pushed her way through the crowd, toward Lizzie's voice. She felt funny when she finally reached Lizzie and saw the shocked look on her face. But Skye was determined to talk to her old friend. She waved Lizzie's essay in the air and said breathlessly, "You left your essay on your desk and I read it. It's so beautiful. Let's be friends. I'm sorry for hurting your feelings. I really didn't mean to. I didn't know you liked Kurt Freeman so much."

Lizzie stared at Skye for a moment. Then she put her arms around Skye in a hug. "I've missed you," she said. "I left my essay on my desk because I just couldn't keep it. It made me too sad to read it and think that we weren't friends anymore." Lizzie looked into Skye's eyes. "I don't know why I got so mad at the dance," she said. "I shouldn't have. I mean, I hardly even know Kurt. He's just someone I had a crush on. Your friendship is more important to me. I've felt awful for the last couple of weeks. I've hardly been able to . . . "

"Excuse me, girls," said the hall monitor. "You should know by now that there's no talking allowed in the halls. I'm going to have to give both of you a pink slip."

"But that's not fair," exclaimed Skye. "We haven't talked to each other in weeks! This is the first time we've . . . "

"If you argue with me I'll have to give you a green slip," said the monitor.

"But, all I'm trying to say is that this is my friend Lizzie," said Skye. "She's my best friend in the world and I haven't had a chance to talk to her in . . . "

"Here's your green slip," said the monitor. She frowned at Skye. "If you keep arguing with me, I'll have to give you *two* green slips," she said.

Skye and Lizzie looked at each other and began to laugh. Then they put their arms around each other and silently walked down the hall to their lockers. Later, seated next to each other on the bus, the words came tumbling out.

"I thought that you were friends with Marcia now, and that you didn't even want to be my friend anymore," said Lizzie.

"No way!" said Skye. "Marcia's on the tennis team. That's how I met her. She's really nice and I can't wait for you two to meet each other. I just know you'll like her. But you know what?"

"What?" asked Lizzie.

"No one could ever take your place!"

"Hey, jerks," said Todd. He stood in the aisle, looking down at the two girls. "I thought you two weren't talking to each other. I thought you had a huge fight over some guy who doesn't like either of you."

"Get lost," said Lizzie.

"Buzz off," said Skye.

"Whoa!" Todd put his hand over his heart. "You girls could give a guy a real complex. Know what I mean?" He ambled off and sat in an empty seat.

"What a nerd," said Lizzie. "Did you know that he's been following me around ever since I asked him to dance at the Harvest Dance? You'd think he'd figure out that girls don't like to be called jerks."

Skye laughed. "Hey! I have a great idea. I'll

have a slumber party this weekend. I'll ask you and Marcia and Nel and Amy. You guys can get to know Marcia better and she can get to know you. It'll be fun. Want to?"

"Sure," said Lizzie. "That sounds neat. Amy's made some new friends in her homeroom. Maybe she could bring them, too."

* * * * *

Skye spent that evening on the telephone with Lizzie. They talked about all the things that had happened in the weeks when they weren't talking to each other. While Skye had gone out for the tennis team, Lizzie had joined the girls' basketball team. Lizzie had purchased some strawberry lipslicker, while Skye had bought a tube of shiny blue eyeshadow. Lizzie told Skye about a boy in her math class named Greg, who kept staring at her. She thought he wasn't bad looking, and best of all, he liked to play basketball. Also, he *never* called her a jerk. In fact, Lizzie told Skye, he usually called her Elizabeth.

"No one *ever* calls me Elizabeth. It's kind of neat," said Lizzie.

Later that night, Amy called to ask Skye if she could bring her two new friends, Karen and Paula, to the slumber party. She explained that they were two sixth-grade girls who had come from Union Elementary.

Skye said, "Sure. Bring them along. I love to meet new people."

When Saturday evening came, Lizzie, Amy, Nel, Karen, Paula, and Marcia arrived at Skye's home. Amy and Nel got to know Marcia and liked her. Skye thought, Everyone seems surprised to find out that such a cute girl was just as afraid as we had been about going to a new school. Karen had more freckles than Skye had ever seen. She knew hundreds of great jokes and she laughed a lot. She was fun to have at a slumber party. Paula was more quiet, but she was just as nice.

As the night wore on, the girls snuggled into their sleeping bags on the living room floor and talked to each other. The moon shone in through the window.

"Do you remember when Bill used to tell you those horrible stories about what the seventh and eighth graders did to the new sixth graders?" Lizzie asked Skye.

Skye began to giggle. "And I believed all of them! Boy, was I dumb," she said.

"Did your brother do that, too?" asked Paula. "Mine told me that they tied your ankles together with kite string, and made you hop down the halls."

"My older sister said that the teachers made you eat chalk if you didn't do your homework," said Marcia. The others laughed at the memories of how afraid they had been that first day at the middle school. It seemed so long ago now. So much had happened.

Nel began to giggle. "Skye," she said. "Remember that first day in gym class when you were embarrassed because you were the only . . . "

"Sh-sh," shushed Skye. "There are some things that aren't worth remembering."

"What's that noise?" asked Paula. The sound of metal clashing and rattling in the driveway came to their ears.

"It's just my brother," said Skye. "He's nice, but weird. His car is falling apart."

The front door opened. Bill came in with a gust of chilly wind behind him. He saw the bodies in sleeping bags on the living room floor. "Hey, Squirt!" he said. "How's it going? Are you girls some of the poor little sixth graders in the middle school? Have they tied your legs together with kite string yet?"

"Sorry, Bill," said Skye. "We've already heard that one. I'm not going to fall for your silly stories anymore. You'll just have to find yourself some new sixth graders to scare."

"What do you mean?" Bill asked with a

laugh. "That's going to be *your* job next year. Goodnight, ladies," he said, and walked back to his room.

"You know, he's right," said Skye. "In a couple of months, it'll be summer again, and we'll all be *seventh* graders."

Just think of those poor little sixth graders next year," said Lizzie. "Wait until we tell them about how they have to lick water off of the floor with their tongues."

"And about how they have to wear their pajamas to class for the first week," laughed Marcia.

"And how they have to clean their plates in the cafeteria," said Nel. "Wow! I can't wait to give those guys the business!"

Skye giggled and said, "You'll never guess what I'm going to do to the new sixth graders next year."

"What's that?" asked Marcia.

"I'm going to be a hall monitor and pass out talking slips."

"You're going to give a million slips to the new sixth graders?" laughed Lizzie. "That should really freak them out!"

Skye shook her head. "No way," she said. "I'll let the new sixth graders talk all they want to in the halls. I'll only give *my* pink slips to the eighth graders!"